I0574368

# LOVE
## *Roulette*
### Book 3 of the Rescued Series:
### Chloe & Daniel Duet

Copyright© 2022 - 2023 by Lyndsay Marie
All rights reserved.
Published by: Lyndsay Marie, September 2023

The characters and events portrayed in this book are
entirely fictitious. Any similarity to real persons, living
or dead, is coincidental and not intended by the author.
That means every bit of it is entirely made up, and any
resemblance to real life is purely coincidental.

No part of this book may be reproduced, or stored in a
retrieval system, or transmitted in any form or by any
means, electronic, mechanical, photocopying,
recording, or otherwise, without express written
permission of the publisher and author.


Cover re-design by: Staci Hart
Editing: Sandra at One Love Editing
Printed in the United States of America by Amazon™
POD services.

If you want to read my other books, keep up with new releases, or buy signed paperbacks, check out my website—

www.AuthorLyndsayMarie.com

Visit me on Amazon —
https://www.amazon.com/author/lyndsaymarie

This book started out as a duet, and can be read in two parts in **What Happens in Vegas** and **Roll the Dice**.

♡ ♡ ♡

To anyone who's ever done something fun, had a few regrets, but everything still worked out just fine in the end...this one's for you!

# ONE

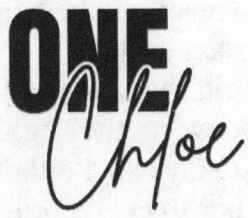

*Chloe*

I would equate my love life to the predictive text of a Magic 8 Ball. "Reply hazy, try again". "Don't count on it". "Outlook not so good". Unfortunately, Magic 8 Balls didn't predict the future. And neither did I. Which was why I never could have guessed in a million years just how accurately my life would end up relating to those fortune-telling phrases. I only wished that Magic 8 Ball could have told me a few months ago that what I thought was going to be a very sweet and heart-felt birthday speech given by my ex, Derrick, as he stood front and center of my favorite restaurant, surround by our closest friends, would turn out to be a dumping of epic proportions. And that he was going to lovingly follow up his speech with one big fat but—and not the kind of butt that Sir Mix-a-Lot rapped about. 'Cause at that moment, I would have gladly taken him putting on an impromptu karaoke session to "Baby Got Back" over what he did to me any day.

My head spun and my ears rang with the highest-pitched noise I'd ever heard as he spoke into the mic. The only important thing I remembered from his entire spewing of bullshit was "Sorry Chlo, this just isn't working for me anymore. I need to find myself." I didn't even have time to react—l like launch myself across the table and beat his ass down.

But, boy, did that asshole find himself, all right. Smack-dab in between the legs of Jensen, my best friend's cousin. Okay, so I didn't have hard proof of that, but given her track record, and apparently his, dinner wasn't the only thing he ate that night.

Such is life, I guess. As pissed off as I was at myself for not seeing his red flags sooner, after all the years of my life I'd wasted with him, I knew I still had time to find *the one*. Eventually. Maybe. But not today. And definitely not by the morning. Nope. What was left of my alone time was going to be about rest and relaxation and scouting out a one and done. Mama needed to be given a big O by a big C.

No sooner had I closed my eyes and lain back on the lounge chair, adult beverage in hand, trying to block out the thoughts about my piece of dog shit ex, than the double doors across the room busted wide open with an explosive echo. My eyes flew open as a huge group of people with at least eight kids and counting came barreling in—all yelling and running in circles, some jumping straight into the pool.

*Fan-fucking-tastic*. So much for rest and relaxation.

Time to move on to plan B—the spa, which was fine by me. I needed a massage, and I'd already planned on getting one at some point anyway. This just pushed things ahead of schedule. So, I pulled up the hotel's website up on my phone, and the first damned thing on their homepage was a notice in bold red letters that they were "Temporarily closed for maintenance. Sorry for the inconvenience."

"Of fucking course," I mumbled quietly to myself. It looked more and more like my time would be spent in the suite…alone. Just me, Netflix on the big screen, and room service dropping off enough fried food for two. One plate for me, another for my feelings—not because I was literally eating for two people.

In the meantime, I popped in my earbuds and set my music playlist to something upbeat. The first song that played was CeeLo's, "Fuck You." How appropriate. A soft *ding* interrupted the song, alerting me of a new text message. I checked my phone. It was Tanner asking me how my day was going and if I was still enjoying my trip.

Ah, Tanner. We'd only been out on our first date prior to my leaving for Vegas, but he seemed like an okay guy. Sweet, gentleman-like, and completely dumbfounded by who he'd agreed to go on a date with. Me. He'd agreed to a blind date through a mutual friend and probably regretted it but didn't wanna piss off the crazy lady, so he'd kept in touch since then. I had to hand it to him, he'd been a trooper during my *slight* breakdown when I witnessed Derrick out with Jensen while we he and I were out on our date. We did make it through the rest of dinner, but then he'd dropped me off at home without so much as a hug or a handshake.

I sighed as more folks steadily trickled in, filling up the pool area—families with kids of all ages and a group of young girls who appeared barely old enough to drink and entirely too mature for their age. A crowd from the local senior citizens' center filed in behind them. *Who opened the flood gates?* Any thoughts I'd had of having the pool somewhat to myself went up in smoke.

A woman with her hair in a disheveled ponytail and dark circles under her eyes headed straight toward me. She had beach bag stuffed to the brim hanging off one shoulder with pool noodles sticking out of the top, a small child in her other arm, propped up on her hip, a second kid clinging to her leg, and a third one running literal circles around her.

I paused my music as she approached because I just knew she was going to talk to me.

"Hi," she said, all smiles and positive attitude as she glared at my cup, probably dreaming of her kid-free days. Personally, I couldn't imagine having that many kids and not staying completely shit faced. "Sorry to bug you, because you look really comfortable, but do you mind if we sit here?" She tipped her chin towards the table and chairs just on the other side of the empty lounge chair beside me acting as a barricade between me and the war zone. "There's no more open tables. We kind of have a big group and need the space."

Clearly, I was not going to catch a fucking break today. "No, of course not," I said with a slightly forced smile, mostly out of pity because I felt sorry for her. "Not at all. Be my guest." As if I were really going to

9

tell her to take her circus and go sit somewhere else. I wasn't *that* mean. I thought it, I didn't say it.

"Thank you," she mouthed as she peeled kids off her limbs and plunked herself and her pool paraphernalia down on the table.

I pulled my bottle of pink champagne out of my bag and refilled my cup practically to the brim, then gulped too much of it in one sitting, way too fast. If there'd been fewer people around, I would have just drunk it straight from the bottle. Then again, all these people were my reason for wanting to get a little tipsy.

Unpausing and turning the volume up on my music, I scanned the room, and—*helllloo, hottie. Where did you come from?* Just when I'd thought there was no hope, the afternoon showed a sign of improving. Not that it was going bad, but my goal of getting laid and having every stupid and ridiculous thought of Derrick fucked out of me started looking more and more promising.

I watched the sexy man across the pool, with dirty-blond hair, tanned, muscular arms bulging out of his white T-shirt sleeves, and brightly colored Hawaiian swimming trunks, as he peeled his shirt off over his head, exposing hell of a lot more tanned skin and muscle that flexed with his every move. My face flushed with heat. It could've been the champagne, but I wanted to give all credit to the stud himself.

One hundred percent, without a doubt, he was the man I wanted to sink my teeth into later…because that was exactly my mission tonight.

Then, as if right on cue—because story of my life—interrupting my inappropriate and wandering thoughts, the music faded out as my earbud dinged again with another text notification.

Tanner. *Shit.* I'd forgotten to respond to him. Not wanting to leave him thinking he'd been abandoned; I did what any good…whatever I might eventually be to be to him—maybe—because we needed to get a few more dates under our belts before I was willing to slap any labels on us…would do. I gave my curly, frizzed-out hair a fluff, readjusted and lifted my boobs in my bikini top, giving them a little shake to even them out, then snapped a selfie with a whole lot of cleavage that took up half my phone screen and sent it to him along with a reply.

Just as I was about to tuck my phone away, it buzzed with another text, this one from Mia, asking if I'd had any luck getting laid. Considering she was the one who'd set me up with Tanner, I knew she felt bad for how our first date had ended.

I rolled my eyes at the thought of Derrick with Jensen and let them land on *fine piece of ass* across the room. I'd been trying to calculate how long I was gonna wait to see if he was going to approach me, or if I was going to break down and go after him first. Because even though my goal was to get laid, I didn't want to come off desperate. But he'd appeared to be an easy enough target. Hell, maybe I was delusional, or he wasn't into red heads…or even women. It was hard to know anymore at first glance.

I texted Mia back: I'd have better luck at a blackjack table at the rate I'm going. Thanks for checking. *And reminding me.*

Once I'd sent my reply to Mia, I realized how much of a pansy I was being, because yes, I was being one. It wasn't like me to just sit around and wait on a dude to chase me down. I was usually the one with the balls making the first move. Time to strap on my big-girl panties, with the hopes of having them ripped off later.

# TWO
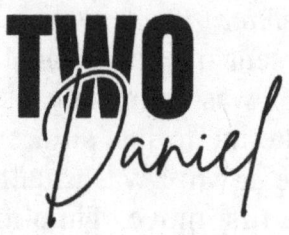

## Daniel

Sin City is a mecca for men like me—single, devilishly handsome—because, yes, I know I am—and up for just about anything with anyone. More specifically, with the female variety. I'd had plenty of guy time. What I wanted was a woman in my bed. So, how was that working out for me so far? Like shit. Why? Not a fucking clue. In the time that I'd been here, I'd laid eyes on only one woman who I thought *might* remotely have bangability potential, and she'd disappeared into the crowd before I could catch up to her.

After Wes left me so he could go sight-seeing and head to the race, I went back to bed to finish sleeping off my hangover. When I eventually woke up from the dead later in the day than I'd anticipated, I'd decided food and a quick dip in the indoor pool was a good place to start. I dialed up room service and ordered a club sandwich and a beer. Once I'd washed down the last of my sandwich with what was left of my drink, I threw on a pair of swim shorts and a T-shirt and headed downstairs, hitting up the bar in the lobby for a fresh, cold one on the way.

"Ho-ly shit," I mumbled to myself as I entered the pool area. I stood just inside the entrance, taking in my surroundings, and debated on going back to my room. My options for redeeming myself after last night's loss dwindled fast. Everyone and their mom— quite literally— who apparently wasn't participating in the marathon, was here. I spotted an empty lounge chair sitting dead-center of a fuck-ton of kids, and from what I could tell, it was the last one available. So, I made a beeline for the chair and tossed my towel down.

I peeled off my shirt and lay back in the chair as I contemplated how I was going kill the rest of the night, when—*who's this and where did you come from*?

Trying not to stare too hard or come across as that awkward creeper across the pool, I picked up my phone as if I were looking at it and discreetly watched the redhead across the room as she sipped on her drink, tapped her foot to whatever music she was listening to, and at one point, readjusted her very large and beautiful boobs, right before snapping a picture of her half a mile of cleavage as she smiled at the camera on her phone. It was a damned shame that pic wasn't coming to me.

She had a flock of kids running and playing wildly around her that occasionally blocked my view, but every now and then I'd catch a glimpse of her and the expression on her face told me she would've rather been anywhere else but had nowhere to go. If I'd had things my way, I was going to change our situation for both of us.

14

Luck was on my side because as the kids parted, I spotted another empty lounge chair beside her, and it had my name written all over it.

I emptied my pockets, covering up my phone and wallet with my T-shirt and walked over to the edge of the deep end of the pool. My intent was to take a quick dip before sliding over and throwing my game on her. The least I could do was get her attention first before being Captain Obvious. When the coast was clear, I dove headfirst into the water. Somewhere between my feet leaving the ground and my head going under, a random fist caught me square in the nuts, sending a shock wave of pain and nausea shooting like lightning through my entire body. If screaming underwater was a thing, I did it…but not without almost choking to death first.

So much for playing it cool.

The kid who'd sucker-punched my junk laughed as I stared him down when I came up for air, then limped my sorry ass to the shallow water. I lifted myself out as gingerly as possible considering my limited movement, and towel-dried off and sat back down in my chair. After allowing myself a few minutes to recover, I rounded up my stuff and decided to man up—just walk or gimp my way over and talk to her—like I should have done from the beginning.

As casually as possible, with a slight falter in my stride, I walked over and stood near the end of her chair, watching her, waiting for her to notice me. She was looking down at her phone with earbuds in both ears. *Great*. But holy shit she was even finer up close. I'd actually kept in the back of my mind the expectation that once I saw her up close, she'd end up not being what I'd made her out to be.

She was better.

When she looked up at me, her hazel-green eyes zeroed in on mine. Then she flashed the most perfect smile, and I came undone...and the dick I'd thought would never work again? The little asshole stirred awake and decided to come alive right then and there, practically eye-level with her.

*Fuck. Now what?* I rubbed the back of my neck trying to come up with something else to say besides "Hi. My apologies for the half-chub." So, I went with another old, bullshit cliché, instead. "Is this seat taken?" *Really smooth, Daniel.*

"Hold on a sec," she said, holding up a finger, pulling out her earbuds. Christ. She didn't even hear me. "Sorry about that. I was trying to drown out all this background noise." She cut her eyes to the side, looking over to the table beside her. "Were you talking to me?"

That wasn't awkward...at all. "I was, actually. I asked if you were using this chair?"

"Nope. Not at all. Take it; it's yours."

Already rejected. *Ouch.* So maybe it was me. But the last thing I wanted was to come across as a total douche-bag. "Actually...I was going to ask if you'd mind if I sat next to you." I gave her a hint of a smile, hoping she'd jump on board...*and maybe my dick later*.

Her eyebrow raised as she gave me a curious look, and then she scanned me from head to toe as if she were on to me. "Yeeeah. You can—" But before the words finished rolling off of her kissable, dark pink lips, some jackass kid came out of nowhere from behind her, grabbed the chair, and slid it backward across the floor, making the most annoying screeching sound as he dragged it away.

*Oh, come the fuck on!* All I needed now was for some other jackass kid to run by and snatch my swim shorts down around my ankles. Yeah, that'd be one more for the big book of humiliation and mortification——me standing with my pants down in the middle of a room full of people, dick standing at half attention in the air.

She stifled a giggle, then busted out into a full-on belly laugh. "Ohmigod. I'm so sorry, but that shit—" she caught her breath to laugh even more. "—was epic."

*Little shit.* He might have been slick, but truth was, I couldn't be mad at her at all for laughing. One day I'd look back and laugh too, but right now, I didn't even care because I got to make her laugh *and* watch her magnificent cleavage jiggle as she did. Score one for me. "Yeah, I guess that was pretty slick."

Then she pointed across the room behind me. "Looks like you just lost your other one too."

I glanced over my shoulder and watched as some big, hairy dude in a Speedo made himself comfortable in what was my seat. *Fucking great.* That left me standing like a moron in front of one of the hottest—no, that wasn't enough—most beautiful women I'd ever laid my sorry eyes on.

17

"Here. Have a seat." She sat up, clearing a spot at the end of her chair, and folded her legs in front of her. "I'll share the bottom half of my chair. There's plenty of room for two on here."

Hell yes, there is. "Thanks, I really appreciate it." I set my stuff down on the ground and straddled the chair, facing her, without hesitation. Her cheeks flushed a hundred shades of red. *Bingo!*

"Shit, I'm sorry. I totally barged over here putting you in a vulnerable position...to be polite. I didn't even introduce myself." I extended my arm to shake her hand. "Dan, by the way."

She hesitated, only slightly at first, then took it. "Chloe."

"Well, Chloe," I said, still holding her warm, soft, tiny, manicured hand in mine. "It's very nice to meet you."

After a pause, she let go of my hand, grabbed her cup, and sipped from it. "A pleasure."

*Oh, you have no idea just how much of a pleasure this could be.* "I'm not intruding on you too much, am I?"

She smiled with the cup still pressed to her lips. Lips that made my heart skip a beat at the thought of them wrapped around my dick. "Nope," she interrupted my fantasy. "Not at all."

"It's okay. You don't have to lie to me. I already know I am, but the real question is, are you okay with it? You can tell me to leave." But not without injury to my pride and a little resistance from me first because I

18

did not want to let her get away just yet if I didn't have to.

Her short auburn hair moved in soft waves as she shook her head. *Jesus Christ.* When in the hell had I ever given a shit about anyone's hair except for my own? Maybe I was assessing how much of it there was for me to wrap my fingers around and pull on later. Yup, that was definitely it.

"Nope. Promise it's okay. I'm just sitting here killing time for nothing, really. And trying not to get socked in the crotch by some kid."

"Wow. You saw that? Huh." I squirmed uncomfortably, trying to readjust myself, as I recalled the very uncomfortable and all-too-recent event. *Well, that's one way to lose a boner.*

"It was kind of hard to miss. Plus, I almost choked to death on my drink from laughing...not at your painful misfortune, just the scene in general."

"Glad you found that shit show entertaining. It wasn't exactly my finest moment."

"Hey!" She leaned forward and smacked my leg. "Give yourself *some* credit. I'll give you at least a six on your dive formation."

"Ouch." I clutched my chest as if her words had hurt. "That's it? Just a six? I took a hit square to the nuts and almost choked to death myself on that nasty-ass pool water. That alone earned me at least a nine." That got another laugh out of her. I made a mental note that I needed to do more of that—make her laugh—because oddly, as seemingly innocent as it was, it was a huge fucking turn-on, and I didn't ever remember anyone's laugh being an actual turn-on. *Like I need another reason to fight off a boner.*

"Fine," she said, waving her hand in a dismissive gesture. "You can have your nine."

I cleared my throat. With any luck, she'd have her own nine soon enough. "Thanks. And you too."

# THREE
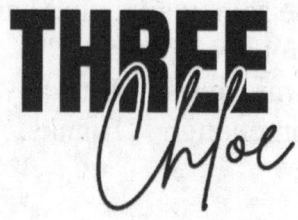
*Chloe*

I fanned my face with my hand. I didn't know if the temperature in the room had risen exponentially or if my own body heat had elevated due to some hormonal or chemical reaction to Dan's voice and his occasional hint of sexual innuendos. Either way, I'd very much enjoyed his subtle—or maybe not so subtle—advances. It was refreshing not having a dude come on so strong without even the slightest restraint. Bonus—he was hot as hell, and he knew how to flirt.

Just as I'd put my cup up to my lips, a ginormous and freakishly hard beachball came flying across the room from out of nowhere, bouncing off the side of my head with a *boing*. I tipped over the edge of the chair. My legs went up, my drink hit the floor. Somehow the beach ball made it back into the pool.

Dan's arm flew toward me, catching me mid-fall, pulling me back upright. "Holy shit, Chloe. You okay? That was a hell of a hit."

The room spun a little, and my vision blurred but slowly returned to normal. "Yeah, no kidding." I rubbed the side of my head and face. "I think I'll live." Okay so getting smacked with the world's largest and hardest beach ball square in the face wasn't the most embarrassing thing that could have happened to me. Neither was spilling my drink all over everything. It was what came next that really caught me off guard and had me turning red.

"Hey," a high-pitched, repulsive-sounding voice said. "Sorry about that."

Dan and I both looked towards the voice. It was one of the girls from the group that'd walked in earlier like a pack of teen wolves. She came up to us from behind Dan and stood between us, her back angled toward me.

"It's fine. Thanks," I said to seemingly no one. She never made eye contact with me and didn't even ask me if I was okay. Despite my wanting to give her a sarcastic *thanks for asking*, I bit my tongue.

She stared down at Dan, who darted his eyes back and forth between me and her with a *what the hell* look on his face. "Yeah, so, me and my friends were wondering," she said, never once taking her eyes off him, "if you'd like to join us in the pool. We promise you won't get hit on with the ball."

Mighty bold move of her. And he wasn't even the one who'd been hit with the ball!

He cleared his throat. "Um. I'm good here. Thanks, though."

Mental fist pump. He wasn't interested in the girl, who was at least ten years younger than me with two-thirds less boobage. I wondered how old he was, anyway? He didn't look or act *that* much older than me, if at all. Hell, maybe he was younger. I'd find out later. Maybe.

Then itty-bitty titties batted her eyes and pouted her lips. "Puh-leeease? I'm sure your sister wouldn't mind if we took you away for a little while to come play."

*What the*—? *Sister*? The Memphis alter ego in me wanted to throw my hair into a ponytail and ask her who the fuck she thought she was talking to. Before I could clear my head enough to speak up, Dan said to her, "I said I'm good here. Thanks."

*Reee-jected. Byyyyyeee.*

She bit her lip harder and looked around uncomfortably.

"He said he's good," I said to her with a hell of a lot of restraint. Cause let's be real, she knew exactly what she was doing before she'd ever approached us. I'd done the same thing once or twice in my life...before I'd known better.

She looked back at her friends, who'd been waiting for her—and Dan—in the pool. Then she turned and walked off without another word.

I blew out a long breath of relief. "Well, that was fun and not at all the least bit uncomfortable."

Dan grinned. "Yeah, you went on the defense for me pretty quick."

"Sorry." No, I wasn't. Dan was my last hope at getting laid, and she was not about to cock block me. "I didn't like the way she came over here knowing we've been sitting two feet in front of each other this whole time. She knew what she was doing."

"Well, I thought it was kind of hot. You defending me, to be clear, not her stupidity." He brushed the side of my face. "You sure you're okay? I mean, not that a beachball is going to leave permanent damage, but that was a helluva hit and you still have a red mark."

"It's not the first time I've taken a ball to the face. I'll be okay."

Dan eyed me suspiciously.

I shrugged. "What can I say? It's a gift."

"Balls to the face. Not your first rodeo. Got it. At least it wasn't me caught in the act of humiliation this time."

"Glad I could take one for the team. And for the record I was talking about sports balls, Dan. Football, basketball, baseball, golf ball. Name it." And male ones too, but that wasn't the point.

"I was just screwing you. With you. Screwing *with* you. Shit. Sorry."

I wish you were screwing me. And hoped even more he fucked as well as he flirted.

"You sure have a way with words."

He shrugged. "Eh, what can I say, it's a gift."

"What other gifts do you have, Dan?"

"Oh, you'll just have to wait and see. I can't just give away all my secrets."

"I look forward to it. Hopefully, we'll get through the rest of the evening without being ambushed. I mean, there's only so many balls a person can take to the face. I'm surprised I haven't come out of it with a concussion by now. Or at the very least knocked a few points off my IQ score."

"Well, I can't help you with your IQ score, but I do know the signs of a concussion. So far, I think you'll be just fine, and the red mark is at least starting to fade some."

"That's reassuring. So what are you, a doctor or something?"

He rubbed the back of his neck. "I am. But don't tell anyone. I like to keep that bit of information to myself when I'm off the clock."

"Noted. So if I need CPR or mouth to mouth, you've got my back?"

"Absolutely."

Sexy and intelligent? *Helllooo, Doctor*.

My phone started pinging with a string of new text message notifications, and I knew exactly who it was.

"You need to get that?"

"Nah. I only have one friend who texts me back to back like that. She's impatiently waiting for me to get back to her." Because the last thing I'd texted Mia was that it'd looked like my luck was about to change when Dan had walked up to me.

"So, Miss Chloe. What is it that you do for a living? If you don't mind me asking. I let you in on my secret, it's only fair I know something about you."

"True. But you know my secret about me taking balls to the face. That's not just something I go around telling everyone."

"Ah, I see. Well, I'll be sure not to tell anyone if asked."

"I'm kidding. I write articles for a magazine. I'd tell you more about it but then I would have to kill you."

He laughed, showing off blinging white teeth and cavernous dimples I probably could have drank from. "No worries. I won't ask. I mean, I'd love to know more about you, but it'll take more than a few hours together to get to know you the way I'd like."

I'd only *thought* Dan had a panty-melting personality. Oh, no. These bitches were burning off. *Okay, Chloe, get it together.* "Well, if you change your mind and decide you wanna know more, I'll be right here." Although, I was kinda glad he wasn't full of questions. I wanted to know just enough about him to get naked without knowing his entire life story.

A twitch of a movement caught my eye. Not like a beach ball to the face movement—because I didn't even see that shit coming. This was the subtle jumping of a—. I internally laughed as Dan readjusted his sitting position. *Oh, honey, you cannot hide something like that from me. Nice try, though.* I might not have been able to see big sports balls flying at my head, but I could spot a hard-on from a mile away any day. I clenched my thighs together, practicing my Kegel exercises, trying desperately to give myself some form of release from the pressure building between my legs. The thought of Daniel's face looking up as he went down on me made me smile.

"What's so funny over there, Miss Chloe. You're grinning like the Cheshire cat."

*Oops*. Must've let my game face slide. "You're paying way too much attention to me, Mr. Dan."

He smirked back at me. "I can't help it. I like what I see."

# F UR

## Daniel

*Holy mother of God.* Flirting with Chloe was like playing with fire—and I welcomed the heat—burn be damned, I was ready.

We bantered back and forth for a little while. I'd say something stupid, she'd laugh, and I did everything I could to hide the bulge trying to grow in my swim trunks.

"I probably should have established this a lot sooner, but are you here alone?" Truth be told, I'd been waiting for some jock-looking dude to pop out of nowhere, snatch me up by my neck, and tell me to piss off. But he hadn't yet, and I couldn't imagine any man with half a brain would leave Chloe unattended for this long. And I didn't think she'd have invited me to sit with her if I were risking getting my ass knocked off. It wouldn't have been the first time for that, either,

"Yup. I sure am…unfortunately." She shrugged.

Unfortunately for someone else. "In Vegas? Surely not." Vegas, as badass of a city as it was, was not the place for a woman like her to be left alone…unless she was a—oh, hell. *Please don't be a prostitute. Please don't be a prostitute. Shit!* Not again. It wouldn't have been the first time I'd accidentally picked up a hooker.

"No, silly man. I'm not alone in Vegas. Just alone at the pool. I'm here on a girls' trip for the weekend. My friends are off running in the marathon tonight. What about you? Are *you* here alone?"

Perfect and *thank fuck*. At least I didn't have to stress about one, having my ass handed to me because I was hitting on someone else's woman, or two, her handing me a bill at the end of the night because I'd had every intention on spending as much time with her as possible. "Guess I'm kind of in the same boat as you." I took a sip of what was left of my, now, lukewarm beer. "I'm here with a friend who's running in the marathon, too."

"Now what kind of friend abandons his runner friend, leaving him to run alone?"

"The same kind as yours, apparently."

"Touché. But in my defense, I was invited on this trip knowing I wouldn't be participating in any form of running. And at least it's two of them together. They can keep each other company. What's your excuse?"

"Don't really have one, I guess. Other than I don't run." About the only marathon I ran was in the bedroom.

"So, what are y'all doing in Vegas? Just here for the race?"

"Something like that. This is just a pitstop. We were in Hawaii for a couple of days before swinging through here."

"Ooh, Hawaii? Sounds exciting. That explains the tan."

I glanced down at my arms. "I didn't think I'd gotten that much sun. Huh, guess I did."

"Yeah, you got a nice tan. I like it."

Her words stirred my dick awake just when it'd started to go down, enough where I could comfortably move without blatantly trying to hide a hard-on. "Thanks. You got a pretty nice tan yourself."

She smiled. "Thank you. I'm a beach girl, myself. Well, mostly weekend trips. I haven't been in months, so I'm surprised it's holding up this long."

"I hardly ever get to a beach and considering I just spent four days in the sun, I'm surprised I didn't walk away with a second-degree burn. Hawaii was my first time at a beach in a long time."

Her head cocked to the side as she looked at me with curiosity. "Wait. Are you and your friend *lovers*?" She raised an eyebrow, and I wasn't sure if it was the thought of two men together or if she was screwing with me...or did she really think I was gay. Surely, she was smart enough to know when she was being flirted with by a straight man.

"Wha—God no." I shook my head. "Do I look...never mind, don't answer that."

She laughed. "I'm kidding. Y'all just on a dudes' vacation?"

I rubbed the back of my neck. "Something like that. I only went to support him while he handled some personal business." I didn't feel inclined to elaborate on his situation any more than that. Our reason for being in Hawaii was difficult enough as it was and not my story to tell.

"And no, you don't, by the way. Was just making sure 'cause you never know now days."

"That's reassuring. Thanks. So, what's with the *y'all*?" I asked, steering our conversation a different direction. "Where are you from?"

She sighed and thought about her answer. "The South."

"That's obvious. You don't have to tell me if you don't want. I was just curious."

"It's okay." She took a sip of her drink. "Where are *you* from, Dan? Is Dan even your real name? Or are you incognito?"

Chloe was turning out to be damned near perfect. She was sexy *and* had a personality with a playful sense of humor? Thank you, universe. "*I* am from the north," I said, mocking her response. "And yes, Dan is my real name...sort of. I gotta keep some parts of me a mystery for now." Because my intent was still to secure a one-nightstand, not get to know the name of her favorite book or childhood pet. Dan would have to suffice for now. Plus, the less I knew about her the better. Knowing led to feelings. The thought alone made me internally shiver because catching feelings was the last thing I needed.

"Well, *Dan*, where are you and your friend heading to next after this?"

"Going back to reality tomorrow."

"Tomorrow? Wow, that's quick." Watching her every move made it hard as hell to focus on our conversation. All I could do was study her and wonder how her lips would taste and feel against mine. I wanted to know what her hands would feel like wrapped around my dick and not that cup. "And where's reality taking you?" she asked me.

I sat up straight, stretching my arms over my head, giving Chloe a better view of the goods, hoping she'd take notice. I inconspicuously watched her as her eyes darted over my bare chest then back down at her drink in her hand. Her face flushed a dark shade of pink. *Bingo.* "We're heading to Illinois."

"Illinois? That's a very cold, harsh reality and a far cry from Hawaii, or here, even," she said.

"No shit. You're telling me. Have you ever been anywhere up north this time of year? Cold is an understatement."

"I've never been to Illinois, but I went to New York for Christmas a few years ago. I actually loved it. It was so magical." Her face lit up as she mentioned New York but very quickly fell flat.

"Yeah, New York is a pretty spectacular place. Though I don't think I could ever live there. So," I said, tipping my chin toward the cup she held up to her lips. "What have you been drinking over there?" I watched her throat move as she swallowed down some of her drink. As if sitting here with her amazing tits three feet from my face wasn't bad enough, just watching her sip gave me a chub and a half. *What a schmuck.*

"Pink                              champagne. It's not very exciting, but it's all I have with me. Want some?" She tipped the cup toward me.

I held my hand up, rejecting her offer. "Think I'll pass on that one. Thanks anyway. I've still got a little bit of room-temperature beer." I gave what was left in the bottom of my bottle a swirl.

"Okay, that's just gross. You wanna get a fresh one? I'm about out of drink myself, now that half of it's on the floor. I could use a refill."

"Now you're speaking my language."

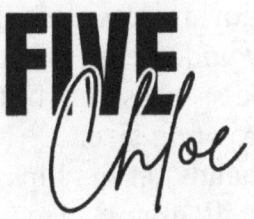

# FIVE
## Chloe

After sitting by the pool admiring Dan's shirtless, muscled-up torso for a couple hours and polishing off the last of my champagne, we'd made the very easy and joint decision to completely vacate the hotel for a while. I needed to take a break from all the heathens screaming and playing, so I could have some unedited adult conversation someplace with a lot less noise. What I really wanted to do was drag him back up to our hotel room, but as it turned out, I was really liking him and didn't want to come off *too* easy—because he made it *really* easy to want to get laid…a *lot*.

We'd gathered our things and made our way out into the hallway where we were instantly greeted by silence as the doors slammed shut behind us.

"Holy shit. I can't believe it's still a damn zoo in there. I thought for sure it would have cleared out somewhat by now."

"You are not kidding. I'm glad you suggested fresh drinks. I don't know how much longer I could have stayed in there."

34

Lyndsay Marie

We turned and stood face-to-face with each other. Sadly, he'd already put his T-shirt back on, but that didn't make him any less sexy. There was no hiding his well-built body underneath a tight-fitting tee…or the obvious bulge under his swim trunks, which I could have sworn had grown in size.

He stood, hands on his hips, towering over my barely five-foot tall frame. His playful blue eyes sparkled, practically begging me for a good time. Little did he know just how much fun I was willing to show him if he stuck around.

"How much free time do you have?"

"Hmm." He rubbed his chin and looked down at his bare wrist as if to check the time, then back at me. "For you? All the time in the world. What's up?"

"Well, since we're gonna get out of here for a bit, I'd like to run up to my room and change clothes really quick."

"Sure. Take all the time you need." He lifted his hand and grazed the pad of his thumb across my jaw. "I'm all yours...all night." His voice dripped with desire and maybe even a hint of a challenge.

My nipples perked at his words. I swallowed hard. "Sounds good. You wanna meet back at the lobby in about ten minutes?" That would give me more than enough time to freshen-up the important things.

"I can do that. You aren't going to run away from me, are you?"

"Me? I would never!" I gave his shoulder a playful shove. He didn't even budge. His body stood firm, like a solid wall of rock-hard muscle planted to the ground.

"Promise?" he said, tucking a loose lock of curled hair behind my ear.

"I guess you'll just have to wait and see." I adjusted my pool bag on my shoulder, turned, and hurried toward the elevator, leaving him standing alone in the hallway.

I couldn't help but smile to myself as I waited because I could feel him staring at me as I walked away. After what felt like an eternity, the reflective gold elevator doors slid opened. I looked back at him one more time. He still hadn't moved, but he had a cocky grin plastered across his face, partially hidden behind his hand that covered his mouth. I waved and disappeared into the elevator.

I pressed the button for my floor. The doors closed shut, and I dropped my head back against the wood-paneled wall, laughing out loud at how my afternoon had taken an unexpected and pleasant turn. I felt like a giddy little schoolgirl who'd just been passed a love note from her secret crush during class.

The ride up ten floors was swift, and I was in our suite in no time at all. Kat and Rowan were off to the race, so I could easily get ready without any distractions or questioning about my plans for the rest of the night. If I'd had more time without him thinking I'd stood him up, I would have taken a shower. Instead, I settled for a quick washup of all the important parts and slathered on some of my favorite Victoria's Secret lotion in hopes that it would mask at least some of the chlorinated smell that lingered on my skin.

Then, I smoothed some dry oil through pool-frizzed hair and touched up my makeup. "Good enough," I said to myself in the mirror. Then, I stripped from my bathing suit, pulled a dress over my head and tugged at the hem, adjusting it in place. Even though it was November, the chilly weather wouldn't stop me from looking cute. I slipped on a pair of wedge shoes, buckling the straps tight around my ankles, and decided I was about as good as I was going to get. It wasn't like this was a date—I didn't even know Dan's last name. Hell, I didn't even know Tanner's last name—,but going out on the town with Dan was as close to a date as two people could get. Without wasting any more time, I grabbed a light cardigan sweater and headed back downstairs.

I made my way around to the lobby, and there were so many people everywhere. Except the only person I didn't see was Dan. I'd been gone less than ten minutes, but it seemed like that'd been long enough for him to change his mind.

"Chloe?" a smooth, warm voice sounded from somewhere close behind me.

I spun on my heels and came face-to-face with Dan. Even with the added four inches of heel under my feet, we were still a few inches from seeing eye to eye. His fresh, deliciously scented cologne hung in the air around us. "Get a look at you, Mr. *GQ*. I'm impressed." Changing from swim trunks and a cotton T-shirt into a pressed linen button-down, navy dress pants, and shined up brown leather shoes, he reminded me of one of those Tik-Tok before-and-after videos. It was enough to make me lose my mind and squeeze my thighs together.

He gave me a cocky grin and my brain disengaged from all things sensible, sending a *zing* straight between my legs. *Damn, body, give me five minutes?*

"Yeah? You think?"

"Oh, I know."

He grabbed my hand and held it out between us, then lifted my arm and spun me around. When I stopped, he wrapped his arm around me pulling me flush against his front, never letting go of my hand. "You, Chloe, are absolutely beautiful."

Heat rose from my chest, creeping up my neck as blood rushed to my face…and everywhere else. "Thank you," I whispered.

All it would have taken was one swift move of me pushing up on my tiptoes and I could have touched my lips to his. And I was confident he would have responded exactly how I wanted. Instead I pulled back, causing him to let me go. "Here I was worried I'd be overdressed."

"Not at all." His eyes wandered down, pausing at the expanse of cleavage popping out of the top of my sleeveless dress, before continuing their scan all the way down and back up. "I didn't think you'd want me to take you out on the town in my swim trunks." Then he pointed to my feet. "Are you going to be comfortable walking around in those shoes?"

Lyndsay Marie

"Absolutely. I'm a pro in these things. Plus, they're strapped on tight, so they aren't going anywhere."

"If you say so." He gave me a questionable look. "So, where to? Have anything particular in mind you want to do? Any place you'd like to go?"

"Nope." Nothing that didn't end with us naked.

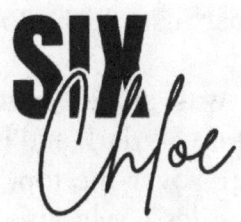

# SIX
## Chloe

We stayed close, barely touching, walking side by side, as we headed toward the exit. I felt myself staying just slightly behind him so I could catch a whiff of his scent as it drifted off him. Maybe it was on purpose; maybe it was subconsciously. Either way, I had no objections to smelling his masculine scent for the rest of the night.

He stopped suddenly. "I have an idea before we head out. If that's okay with you?"

"Of course. We can do whatever you want." *Like go back upstairs and fuck like animals.*

A mischievous grin spread across his face. "You up for a quick drink?"

*Damn.* So much for breaking the bed. "Um, sure." I was already feeling damned good from the almost entire bottle of champagne I'd smashed at the pool, but I'd been a few hours since I'd started drinking. Besides, I didn't come here to quit now. I came to Vegas to have a hell of a time, and that was exactly what I'd planned to do. Meeting Dan seemed to be the start of it.

All hope wasn't lost yet.

40

"Good. Come on." He rested his hand at my lower back, guiding me forward slightly ahead of him and led us into a bar just off the lobby beside the main entrance.

The room was small, barely big enough for twenty people, but it was dark and intimate and swanky. Nothing short of over-the-top. The floors were reflective black tiles. Massive sparkling crystal chandeliers hung overhead, and glittery granite countertops ran the entire length of the room. The expansive back wall behind the bar was one ginormous, back-lit mirror lined and stacked with every bottle of liquor known to man.

We walked up to the counter and were greeted by the only other person in the room with us—the bartender. "Good evening, what can I get for you two?" he asked as he approached.

Dan leaned over, propping himself up against the counter, and looked down at me, or maybe my boobs. "You up for taking a shot? I know you've gotta be feeling pretty good already. But I figured I'd catch up with you before we head out."

I smiled and leaned against the bar, mirroring his stance but also for support. "I' still feeling pretty damned good, but I never turn down a challenge."

"Never?"

"Not yet." Which was true. If there was one thing I knew about myself it was if I were ever dared to do something, shit would get done. Sometimes my luck and limits were tested, but I'd yet to back down.

"Interesting. I'll have to tuck that little tidbit of info in my back pocket for later use." He tapped his knuckles against the granite counter. "You have a favorite?"

"Challenge?" That got a hearty laugh out of him. Enough for me to see a dimple on each cheek that I hadn't even noticed until now. *Panties wet? Check.* Note to self: don't wear any next time.

"No, Chloe. Favorite shot."

*Duh.* The fact that this man had the ability to completely disengage my brain of all common sense scared the crap out of me, yet the unfamiliar feeling of letting my guard down was somewhat refreshing. "Actually, I do. It's called a buttery nipple."

He cringed at my response. "Such a chick drink."

"Call it what you want, but it gets the job done. Since you're so manly, you pick."

He raised an eyebrow. "You sure about that?"

"Oh, I'm always sure. If we're going to do this, let's do it the right way or your way. Whichever is better."

He smiled again and ordered two shots of top-shelf Patrón.

*Well, that's another way to do it.* "Should make for an interesting night." I said it more as a mumble to myself, but he'd heard me loud and clear.

"You're telling me. I had way too much fun, we'll call it, last night. We didn't get back to our suite until almost four this morning. Then I slept until almost that same time this afternoon."

"Same here. What'd y'all get into?"

"Karaoke. Some place here, actually. There's a club on the other side of the casino. We got there pretty late, though."

"Really? We were there too."

"Oh yea? Did you sing?" He asked, his tone playful and mocking.

I rolled my eyes. "You can call it that. I only do it with a few drinks and moral support."

"Interesting. I don't remember seeing you."

"Well, I was there, all night. When did y'all get there?"

"I don't really remember what time we got there. We just hopped off the plane, dumped our luggage, and headed back out." He shifted to face me, inching just slightly closer. "It's too bad we didn't get the chance to cross paths last night."

*You're telling me.* "Really? And why's that?" I wanted so damned bad to reach out and touch him—any part of him. I wanted to know what his body would feel like underneath my fingertips—but I didn't do it. I kept my hands to myself. I still couldn't bring myself to pass the first move. *Why, Chloe, why?* It wasn't like I was out of my element. *This* was my element. *He* was my element.

Dan didn't have to come up with an answer on the spot as to why he'd wished we'd met sooner. The bartender appeared and laid down two napkins in front of us and set our shot glasses down on top of them, along with a saltshaker and two limes. "Enjoy."

"Thank you," We said in unison.

He nodded and went back to working on a computer at the other end of the bar.

"I hope you're ready for this."

"I'm sure I'll be okay. I've shot tequila before. This isn't my first rodeo."

He winked. "Not like this." Before I could ask what the hell he was talking about, he licked the back of his hand and sprinkled some salt on the wet spot. Then, just as fast as he'd made his entrance into my world, he grabbed my hand and slowly licked the back of it, then covered the wet spot in salt. "Now hold your arm out."

"What?" I didn't even try to hide the confusion that was written all over my face. "My arm?"

"Yes, your arm." He handed me my shot glass and picked his up. Never letting go of my hand, he held my arm in the air with the hand that had the salt on it and positioned it near his mouth. He closed his eyes as he moved his mouth to my hand, just near the edge of the salt, pressing a soft, lingering kiss on my skin. His lips on me sent chills all the way to my toes. So much for my clean-shaven legs. "Now, hold it right there," he said in a volume low enough for only us to hear. "Don't move."

I held my breath. My arm was suspended in the air with my hand barely brushing the corner of his mouth, as I clenched my shot of tequila in the other. Any tighter and I could have broken the glass.

He put the back of his own hand with the salt on it near my mouth. "You know the rules?"

I nodded. "Yes." I think. But this was apparently a new a version of an old game.

44

"Just follow my lead. Lick. Drink. Suck. I think you can handle that."

*Holy mother of God and sweet baby Jesus.* Where in the hell had this sexy motherfucker been my entire adult life? I mean, I'd been with some seriously hot men, so that wasn't the issue. I'd also been with some slick-ass men who were thought they knew what they were doing. But Dan *knew* what he was doing without having to tell me. He exuded confidence that consumed me. *That* was my weakness. "Got it," I whispered forcefully.

He kept his eyes locked with mine. "Cheers to new...friends, new adventures, and new challenges."

"Cheers."

Then, without missing a beat, he licked the salt off the back of my hand and tossed back his shot.

I hadn't even moved. I was too busy watching him lick me. My hand. He licked the back of my hand and I was ready to jump his dick.

I sucked in a sharp breath and held it until my lungs burned. Not yet, I told myself. Patience was never my virtue, but I was gonna practice it hard, for now.

"Chloe?" He raised an eyebrow. "Are you going to take your shot?"

I swallowed hard, snapping out of my fantasy of me riding him on the counter while the bartender watched. "Yeah. Of course. Cheers." I repeated his movements by slowly licking the salt off the back of his hand, then downing my shot. I plopped my shot glass down on the counter with a *thud.*

He picked up a lime wedge and gently touched it to my lips. "Bite it."

I did, only with slight hesitation, because my throat and chest were on fire. Then I took the other lime and did the same to him, holding it up for him to bite.

"Jesus Christ," he mumbled under his breath after removing the lime from between his lips. He wiped his mouth with the back of his hand. "We need to get the hell out of here. Now."

# SEVEN
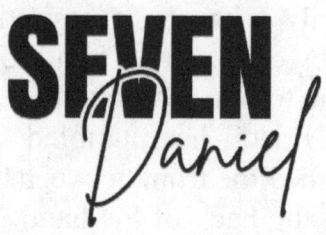

I knew if I didn't get Chloe out of that bar, or entire hotel, stat, I was going rip that way-too-short-ass of a thing she called a dress over her head and bury my dick balls-deep inside of her or bust a nut in my pants trying. It took every ounce of self-control I had within me not to drag her back upstairs. The fact that I didn't frustrated the hell out of me because she was supposed to be like the rest of them—fuck 'em and leave em was the name of the game. Avoid small talk, nothing too personal—get in, get mine, and go.

My dick had barely gone down since I saw her, which told me I was on the right track...at first. But the fact that I hadn't actually tried to do anything about it yet had me questioning my own self-made hierarchy of needs. I was fully convinced Maslow had it all wrong, in terms of basic needs, until now.

We stepped outside into the public eye. The sun had all but disappeared, and a chill hung in the air which meant it was only going to get colder as the night wore on. Chloe was wearing practically nothing in a sleeveless minidress that showcased half a mile of fuckable cleavage. She had what looked like a paper-thin cardigan hung delicately over her arm. "It's probably going to get kind of chilly for you, being from the South and all. Did you want to grab a heavier jacket?"

"Nah. I think I'm okay for now. We're probably not going to get very far anyway with everything blocked off. I can come back and grab one if need be."

"If you insist. I guess if you change your mind, I can always do the gentleman-like thing and give you my coat. But don't expect me to use it to cover any water puddles for you to step on." Not that I didn't want to be a total gentleman to Chloe—despite my animalistic drive to fuck her senseless, which, thankfully, she couldn't read my mind—but this was a high-end sport coat that'd cost more than our hotel room for the weekend.

She looked at me with a shocked expression, threw her hand over her chest, and gasped. "You mean you wouldn't do that for me?"

"Oh, no." I smiled. "I'd just pick you up and throw you over my shoulder."

"That works too." She laughed at my admission, seemingly not realizing how serious I was about carrying her, and I loved her naivety. Everything about her, especially the way she laughed. It warmed me up on the inside.

"So, Miss Chloe, where to?" We stood on the sidewalk at the end of the hotel drive and looked up and down the Strip. The fun half had been barricaded for the marathon.

"How long do I really have with you? That might help us determine what we get into."

Oh, I had a damned good idea what I wanted to get into, and she was standing beside me. "All night. Remember?"

"Really? All night? You mean you don't have any other plans, like meeting your friend after the race?"

"Nope. Not a one. I'm sure he'll go back to the room and crash. I doubt he'll want to meet up. What about you? You're not joining your girlfriends?" *Please say no. Please say no.* I knew chances of her staying with me through the entire night was slim since she was here on a girl's trip. Surely, her dedication was to them and they'd be expecting to meet up with her at some point.

"Nope. No plans. I told my girls to go, have fun, I'd catch up with them later or tomorrow. I figured since those two had been practicing for this race for at least six months, I'd give them their moment of glory."

"Hmm, interesting. Let's go this way and see where the sidewalk takes us." Halle-fucking-lujah. Chloe was mine. Well, eventually. Maybe. For the past few hours, I'd kept my hands to myself and resisted the urge to hump on her like a horny dog. Surprisingly, to me, what I wanted to do more than anything was reach over and hold her hand or put my arm around her shoulders and tuck her into me. Instead, we walked comfortably beside each other, both of my hands shoved safely in my pants pockets, away from her curvaceous little body. Plus, I still didn't entirely know her motives, or what she wanted. So far, she seemed to just be along for the ride.

We continued walking a short way down the strip before we'd decided to take a detour onto a less populated street just a few blocks over.

"Probably should have established this hours ago," she asked, looking up at me through her thick, jet-black eyelashes, "but *you're* not seeing anyone...are you? You're not like tied down?"

I held back a smirk at the thought of being tied down by her or me tying her down. "Nah. I prefer to remain...what's a nice way to put it...habitually unattached?"

"Wow. Not just unattached, but habitually unattached? That sounds pretty serious. How come you made a habit out of it? Not a fan of relationships?"

"Ehhh...just a personal preference. Keeps things easy."

"So, you're a serial dater, then?"

"Not exactly. I don't really date either. Let's just say I have my needs met on a regular basis."

"Interesting. So, when's the last time you had a solid, long-term relationship? Or have you ever?"

I slowed my stroll and rubbed my chin. Not that I had to think about it, but it'd been a while.

"That long, huh?"

I smiled. "It's been a few years." Hell, it'd been more than a few years. Close to ten, actually.

"And what happened with her? If you don't mind me asking."

I shook my head. "I don't mind at all." Though, I was slightly hesitant since I wasn't much for relationship talk. But Chloe had a way about her that was somewhat comforting; she was easy to talk to, so I went for it. I gave her my sob/failed-relationship story, the one that led me into serial dating. "Julia," I said. Just saying Julia's name out loud caused a pang in my chest. Not because I missed her. I just didn't do a whole lot of reminiscing about her or us. When she walked out, I'd closed the door on her and my heart. "We grew up together—high school sweethearts, prom king and queen. All your classic fairy-tale crap packaged into one seemingly everlasting relationship. We met in middle school and dated from high school into college. All the way until I was up to my asshole in stress and debt six years into med school. I was planning on asking her to marry me after graduation. But she met someone else—a classmate at the time, actually—and she decided he was a better fit for her than me."

Chloe was silent for an uncomfortably long minute, then said, in the cutest, drawn-out Southern accent, "Well, shit. I wasn't expecting all that."

"Deep, yeah? You asked." I nudged her playfully with my elbow.

"I sure did. Walked right into that one. I'm really sorry to hear that. That was shitty of her. Hell, after that I wouldn't want to get into a relationship either."

"Eh. It's all good." It was a relief to be able to talk about Julia and not feel anything toward her—good or bad. Even better that I hadn't seen her since. She was either avoiding me like the plague or I was just one lucky bastard. "I mean, think about it. I could be shacked up with her, surrounded by God only knows how many kids by now. After she left me, I was crushed for sure. But it put a lot of things into perspective. We just weren't meant to be. She's married to him, I think, living the life of her dreams, I'm sure. Besides, if things had gone differently, I wouldn't be here with you. So, I'm okay with life's mysterious ways of working out." I brushed her soft hair away from her face. As much as I'd thought about going hard on Chloe and fucking her brains out ever since I'd laid eyes on her, I really wanted to just touch and taste her. To feel her full, burgundy lips against mine. Instead, I rubbed my hands together and said, "Now it's my turn."

"Oooh? You're gonna question me now? This should get interesting."

"Yuuup. I noticed earlier your mood changed when you talked about that time you visited New York. What happened there?"

She picked at invisible lint on her cardigan, which she'd already put on, but still somehow managed to leave the swell of her breasts exposed. "Nothing, really. Just a misunderstanding. That's all."

*My ass.* Paying attention to detail was half of what I did for a living. I gently bumped her shoulder with mine so I wouldn't knock her off-balance. "Come on. I told you about my majorly failed happily ever after. Tell me about yours. I promise I won't hold any past fuck-ups against you."

She looked up at me. "What makes you think it has anything to do with love?"

"Because no one talks about being in New York City at Christmastime and gets sad."

She huffed. "Fine. His name was Derrick. We were together for a couple of years. Nothing that compared to your love story, but I thought he was the one. Manhattan was the last vacation we took together as a couple. I was so stupid. I actually thought he was going to propose to me at the Rockefeller Center. When he didn't, I figured it was because it would have been too cliché since there were several other couples already there being proposed to. We got home and things went back to normal. A few weeks later, a bunch of us got together for my birthday. He went all out for it too—reserved a private banquet room at my favorite restaurant, had the whole thing catered. Then towards the end of the night, he got on the microphone for a special announcement and dumped me right in front of our friends and waitstaff. He set the mic down and walked out without another word."

You could have cut the silence between us with a knife after that story. She breathed a long sigh of relief.

"And you haven't talked to him since? He didn't even try to reach out and apologize or come crawling back on his hands and knees begging for forgiveness?"

That made her giggle. "Nope. Not a word. He's way too good for that." She shrugged. "I've moved on. I actually just went out on my first date since he dumped me, and you wouldn't believe it, but Derrick was at the same damn restaurant on a date with my best friend's cousin."

What in the hell was wrong with this guy? "Jesus, Chloe. What a pathetic douche bag. I'm really sorry." I reached out and grabbed her hand. *Finally.* Now I had a reason to touch her without coming across like a douche bag myself. Despite the cold, her hand was warm and soft and practically disappeared in mine. I gave it a squeeze, then spun her to face me. She had tears in her eyes. *Shit.* I hated it when women cried. I stepped forward, pulling her into me and wrapped my arms around her. *Fuck* she felt good in my arms even if she was seemingly on the verge of a breakdown. But she was the first woman I'd held in a long time just for the sake of holding her. She didn't return my embrace. Instead, she kept her arms to her side, but she didn't need to. All I wanted was for her to know I was there for her, if she needed me, and not entirely for personal gain.

Reluctantly, I pulled back, holding her at arm's length, and searched her teary eyes. Yup, her ex really did a number on her, but I had an idea—something to get her mind off him and hopefully cheer her up. She didn't deserve that kind of pain. I knew exactly what it was that would make her feel better, and it wasn't me. "You know what you need?"

She sniffled, wiping her face. "What?"

A kiss was the first thing that came to mind. Not that that would have been the most appropriate moment, but it sure as hell couldn't have been the worst thing I could have done to her. Instead, went for the obvious second best thing. "Ice cream."

# NINE
## *Daniel*

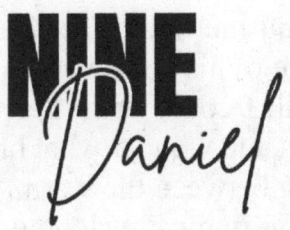

That was the first time I'd talked about me and Derrick openly to anyone in a long time, and damn, it felt kinda good—like a weight I didn't know I'd been carrying around had been lifted off me. I'd talked about it to Rowan and Katie, but they were there when it all went down. It wasn't something I'd really wanted to keep bringing up. Talking to someone on neutral ground was a different feeling.

"This is perfect," I said, spooning another heap of chocolate and peanut butter ice cream from my cone and into my mouth. After having that conversation about our exes, I think we both needed this. Dan didn't hesitate when he'd spotted this place and practically dragged me down the street to a little mom-and-pop ice cream and candy shop. I'd forever be grateful for it—for him.

We'd overloaded our waffle cones, already overflowing with double scoops of ice cream, with more toppings than what should have been consumed by any one human in a single sitting and sat at a small dinette table for two next to the window. "Apparently I needed this more than I realized. Thank you."

"You and me both," he said, his tongue traced around the edge of his waffle cone.

It was all I could do to keep from staring at the way he licked it and wonder what his cold tongue would feel like sliding between the warmth of my legs.

"And you're most welcome, Chloe."

I smiled at his sweet and thoughtful sentiment. "Seriously, it's very much appreciated." I sucked in a deep breath and slowly blew it out. "I haven't really talked about Derrick much, even to my best friends. They were there, so they stood as witness to the whole thing and how embarrassed I'd been. It felt kinda nice retelling my story to someone who doesn't really know me."

He reached across the table and took my hand in his. "I'm happy to be here for you. Feel free to vent all you want. Or get more ice cream if you think you'll need it." He smiled.

"I appreciate it, but I'm okay for now. No more Derrick and definitely no more ice cream."

We finished our dessert, cleaned up our mess, and headed back out to the street. *Shit!* It'd gotten cold. I knew better than to wear such a skimpy dress, but hell, I'd only had one thing in mind when I put it on, and I was beginning to think I'd really misread Dan's intentions...or maybe they'd changed since spending more time with me?

A chill ran through me, causing me to shiver. I wrapped my cardigan tighter around my chest and hugged myself.

He threw his arm around me, rubbing up and down my arms, as he leaned into my ear and whispered, "Told you so."

I drew back and playfully smacked his chest. "Yeah, well, you also told me you'd give me your jacket to keep me warm. So, man up. I'm cold."

He smiled as he shrugged off his blazer, showing off his muscles straining against his long-sleeved button-down shirt in the process, and placed the jacket over my shoulders. "I am a man of my word, Chloe. How you feeling? Sobering up? Buzzed? You want another drink?"

Miraculously, my buzz had worn down to almost nonexistent. Probably from finally getting some form of food into my stomach. "Depends. Are you gonna pull some sexy stunt like you did at the bar earlier?" I slipped the word "sexy" in there to describe his previous stunt because I wanted him to know that shit he did was in fact sexy and I savored each and every one of his moves, and I wouldn't mind if we did it again.

He grinned. "Depends. Did you enjoy it when I licked you?"

"You have no idea." Hell, my panties were still wet from the moment he'd licked my hand at the bar when we took our first shot. "I spotted an outdoor walk-up bar a few doors down. Why don't we go find out?"

Without hesitation, we walked up to an open window on the side of a restaurant-bar. It reminded me of Silky's on Beale Street back in Memphis. "Shots? Or would you rather have something you can sip on?"

"How about both? Since we don't have anything planned for the rest of the night." At the rate we were going, we'd either never make it back to the hotel or we'd end up waking on a park bench. Either way, I had a feeling neither one of us would remember much of it.

"I really like the way you think."

We ordered two more shots of something not top-shelf—Dan's pick—and two big-ass fruity frozen drinks—my choice. Taking the shots this time was not nearly as sexy as before. There was no licking, no lingering kiss on the hand, but they still did the trick.

I felt myself swaying as we stood side by side watching the world go by, internally contemplating what to do next. Dan grabbed me and held me with one arm, his drink in the other hand, steadying me.

Our faces were inches apart. I could smell fresh liquor and raspberry on his breath, or maybe it was my own.

*Finally.*

He was going to kiss me.

This was it—that cliché moment in all those cheesy romance movies I'd seen where the girl finally gets to kiss the guy. I'd been waiting for this since he'd sat down in front of me at the pool. Okay, so that wasn't a very long time, but I knew what I'd wanted from him from the get-go.

I tried blinking away my steadily blurring, buzz-induced vision before closing my eyes.

Instead of his full, kissable lips touching mine, he let go and pulled away.

*What the?*

"Let's go sit down somewhere. I noticed a place on the way over here. But first, there's something I need to do."

So that was not what I'd imagined happening at all. "Oh?" He handed me his cup and got down on one knee in front of me. "What the? What are you—"

"You'll see." He fidgeted with the straps of my shoes. "Hold still and try not to spill anything on me. I'm running out of clothes to wear. You've already confiscated my jacket. There's not much left for me to give away."

Good to know and that was just as fine by me.

"I'm taking your shoes off," he said, "before you tip over and faceplant the sidewalk. If I'm going to get you drunk, the least I can do is make sure you're safe."

I smiled so hard my cheeks burned. Between his devilishly handsome features and thoughtful gestures, I didn't think my smile would ever fully leave my face. I couldn't ever remember meeting a man or being around one who took care of me with such thoughtful consideration as Dan had, even in the few short hours we'd known and been around each other.

His fingers deftly worked the tiny buckles around my ankles, loosening the straps, allowing me to step out of my shoes.

*Shit.* It was a relief having my feet in a flat position, but damn, the concrete sidewalk was freaking cold. I thanked him anyway for knowing exactly what I'd needed.

As he stood up, his lightly traced his fingertips along the back of my ankles, up my ankles, behind my knees, finally to the back of my thighs, stopping just below the hem of my dress.

I let out a shiver.

He stood up, towering over me, and exhaled a cloud of breath as if he'd been holding it in. I knew I'd been holding mine.

"You're welcome." Then he grabbed his drink out of my grip, turned his back to me, and leaned down. "Hop on."

"You can't be serious?"

He handed me my shoes over his shoulder. "Hop on my back. I'll carry you. You're barefoot. I'm not about to let you walk the streets of Vegas without shoes on."

I bit into my bottom lip. I wasn't sure if him carrying me piggyback was a smart idea. "You sure?"

"Absolutely, but the sooner the better. I don't know how much longer I can bend like this before I fall over myself."

I grabbed his shoulders as best I could, with a drink in one hand, my shoes in the other, and climbed on to his back. He carefully stood up straight. I wrapped my legs around his waist, holding on for dear life, just in case. 'Cause if he went down, I was going with him...or at least using him as a landing pad.

"Hold on but try not to choke me...unless you're into that kinda thing."

"Ohmigod." I playfully but lightly smacked his shoulder.

He shrugged. "Just checking. You never know."

Don't get me wrong, I'd done some freaky shit, but choking was a hard pass. He'd find out if he ever tried. Or if we ever got to that point. "Where are we going?"

He lifted one of our drinks, gesturing to seemingly nothing behind us. "That way."

I looked back behind us. "Where?"

"Exactly."

We walked just a few feet away to an inconspicuously placed garden between two brick buildings that if you weren't looking for this place or didn't already know it was there, you'd never have known it existed.

We made our way through the tiny, gardened area. I carefully slid down Dan's back trying to keep my dress from riding up and sat down on a bench. We were all the way in the back of a dark courtyard in front of a brick wall in the farthest corner. The whole space was void of all light, except for a beam of light that poured in from the streetlights at the edge of the garden, just barely reaching our feet.

We were completely out of view but could still see everyone walking by.

It was the perfect hiding spot.

I dropped my shoes to the ground in front of me and took my drink from Dan. "This is really dark," I said, tucking my legs under me in an effort to warm up a little. I silently cursed myself for not wearing jeans and a cute top. But nooo, I just *had* to wear a damned dress.

Dan sat down beside me and took a sip of his drink. "What's the matter? You scared?"

I cocked my head to the side. "I don't know. Should I be?" Okay, so I wasn't the least bit concerned for my safety. Should I have been? Maybe. I mean, I did essentially run off into the night with a stranger—not the dumbest thing I'd ever done—without so much as leaving any kind of evidence to be found or telling anyone where I was going. Not to mention, I'd realized a while back that I'd left my freaking phone in the suite in my haste to get ready. At least I was on security cameras, so if something did happen, it'd give police a starting place.

Plus we were in an area that if I'd talked loud enough, I'd be heard, so yelling would definitely get people's attention.

So, no, I wasn't the least bit scared.

Still horny as fuck, though, and still not willing to pass the first move to do anything about it.

He draped his arm around my shoulders and inched closer to me until my knees were touching his thigh. "Absolutely not. You're perfectly safe with me."

"Good to know." I wrapped both my hands around my cold cup, suddenly nervous. I'd been in this scenario a hundred times before, so why was this any different? I didn't have a clue other than something about Dan felt different, but I was willing to ride it out to find out if it meant me riding him before the end of the night.

Then he shifted to face me, catching me off guard when he grazed the back of his finger against the swell of my cleavage, leaving goosebumps in its trail. Ice water dripped off the cup onto my boob, trickling down between my cleavage. "Now that we've established you aren't in fear of your life around me I have a question for you."

"Go for it."

"I'm curious, Chloe, who were you sending pics of these fantastic tits to earlier at the pool?"

I had to think about that one for a second, not because I'd sent out so many boob pics that I couldn't keep up, but because my memory had become significantly impaired over the last little bit.

Then I remembered what picture he was referencing since I hadn't actually sent out any boob shots recently. "Oh, yeah, uh, Tanner. He was just checking on me to see how my trip was going."

Dan skimmed the bottom edge of his cold, wet cup across my other boob, letting the water drip down. "Tanner? And he's not your boyfriend?"

*Shit.* I took a huge swig of my own drink. "Nope. Not all. He's the one I told you about that I just went on a first date with when I saw my ex out with someone else. It's too soon to be serious." And after tonight, probably never would be because spending time with Dan only confirmed one thing—I was not ready to settle.

"He's a lucky bastard."

"What makes you say that?"

"Because," he said, as he tipped his head down, planting a soft kiss on the top of my boob on the wet spot where his finger and the cup had been. *I got another wet spot you can kiss.* "He's probably seen these, even if it was only in a picture."

I sucked in the cold air night, suddenly flushed with a rush of heat mixed with desire that went straight between my legs. My head rolled back as his tongue traced a line to the other side. I wanted to throw my drink to the ground and straddle his lap right here.

I knew for a fact he'd been hard more times than not throughout the night. You couldn't hide a dick like that. Especially not from me.

When he tried to move away, I grabbed the back of his head, threading my fingers in his hair, and pulled him back into my chest. I needed *some* action. *Anything.*

I felt him smile against my chest. "You like?"

It was all I could do to breathe out the words "Whatever you do, don't stop."

# NINE
## Daniel

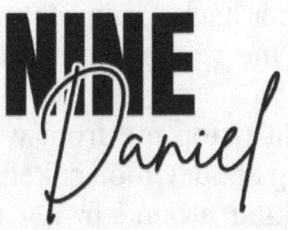

*My God.* Chloe's skin smelled like heaven mixed with vanilla, bourbon, and cinnamon, and I wanted to drink every inch of her to the last drop. I'd noticed how sexy she'd smelled when I'd whispered in her ear earlier, and now, with my face planted between her perfect, warm tits, I couldn't get enough of her.

Christ, I could have busted a nut in my pants just breathing her in.

I couldn't help but wonder what she'd smell like with my nose buried between the lips of what I could only assume was the most perfect-looking pussy I'd ever lay my eyes on.

*In due time.* At least that's what I kept telling myself.

My goal when I'd walked out of my hotel room was to get laid. It'd been over a week, and I just wanted to get my dick wet.

Then Chloe appeared.

I knew I wanted her, but she did not come across an easy target. I was confident, though, until I looked

Lyndsay Marie

into her eyes. Then we'd spent so much time at the pool just talking and getting to each other, I couldn't bring myself to take her back to my room.

She had me wrapped around her finger and had no idea.

That didn't stop me from wishing. And when I wasn't dreaming about Chloe naked, the rest of my time was spent walking around trying to hide the big-ass bulge in my pants. It was even worse now that I'd had the tiniest, teasing taste of her…and nowhere even near where I really wanted my tongue to be.

She gripped and pulled my hair as I lightly kissed and licked and sucked on the exposed area of her luscious breasts. All I could picture was how her perfectly manicured feet would look with her ankles resting on my shoulders as I pounded my cock into her, while her tits bounced, and her mouth formed the perfect *O* as she came all over me.

The more time that'd passed, the dirtier my thoughts about the two of us together became…and the more I really liked her, too.

I felt a firm tug at my hair, pulling me to look up.

"Kiss me," she said, breathlessly. "Please, Dan. I really want you to kiss me."

And I wanted that too, so fucking much.

But I withheld from going full force, no holds barred on her and answered on instinct without even thinking. "No." Which was a hell of a lot easier said than done.

A look of shock and borderline horror etched across her face as she drew back. I knew that look.

67

Pretty sure I'd seen that expression before at least once in my past.

*Mayday, Mayday!*

She was either going to cuss me out or kick me in the face.

"No? What do you mean *no*?" Her voice was surprisingly a lower octave than I'd expected.

*Shit.* I just knew I'd totally blown it with her.

I sat straight up, slightly out of her reach, and downed some of my drink, thinking carefully before I opened my mouth to speak again. "Trust me, Chloe, I want to kiss you like a mother fucker. You have no idea."

"Then do it."

"I can't."

"Well, why not?" She looked even more confused. If she didn't think I was into men before, I was sure she did now. "What's the problem? You seem to have enjoyed kissing my cleavage. How are my lips any different?"

*Fuck.* I'd never felt so torn in my life. My mind was telling me to slow down with her, but my raging hard-on clearly didn't get the memo. "Look. All I've wanted to do since I laid my eyes on you at the pool was one, get my hands and mouth on you *and* your tits, and two, fuck every inch of you every way possibly known to man. Which, I'm not gonna lie, was exactly my goal tonight before we met. I mean, that's what I do. I'm a player. But, as it turns out, I've really enjoyed your company and I'm starting to kind of like you for more than just a piece of ass. I think you deserve better than that."

Well, if nothing else, she'd think I was a pussy for backing out on the opportunity.

Instead, she smiled. "Really? You mean that?"

I leaned back against the bench, breathing a sigh of relief, relieved that I wasn't going to take a second hit to my jewels in the same night.

"Yes, really. You're the most beautiful woman I'm pretty sure I've ever seen and you're so damn sweet. As much as I'd love to take you back up to my hotel room and knock the bottom out of it, if I'm being totally honest with you, I'd really rather control myself and enjoy your company for a while...if that's okay with you."

I thought for sure she was going to run at this point. My confidence tanked by the minute.

Instead, she rested her delicate hand on top of my own, which I'd planted firmly to my thigh. "Okay, then. I can respect that and thank you for respecting me. Slow it is."

I kissed the top of her head. "And do not mistake my abstinence for my not being attracted to you because holy fuck, I am going to come hard and fast at some point when I jerk off to you later."

Surprisingly, that made her laugh. *Score another one for me.* She didn't seem repulsed by my admission that I was going to jerk off to thoughts of her...and no doubt, more than once.

"Tell you what," she said. "Until we figure out what we're gonna do, let me make a deposit into your spank bank then."

"I'm listening."

"Get your camera ready." She set her drink down while I fished my phone out of my pocket as quick as I could, trying not to drop it and turned the camera on in record time. "Whatever you do, do not get my face."

"Promise." Then, with little to no effort, she pulled the front of her dress down, exposing her large, luscious tits, with a bounce.

My mouth watered when her nipples hardened as the cold air hit them. "Holy shit."

She held open my jacket. "You'd better hurry up. It's cold."

"Well, it's working to my benefit. Don't move."

She let out a soft giggle. Every sound that fell from her lips was music to my ears. While I'd thought about all the things I wanted to do to that mouth of hers, I turned the camera flash off, as to not attract any attention to us, and switched the night mode feature on—thank you, technology—and centered her chest to take up the as much of the screen as possible. I snapped as many pics as I could—sans Chloe's face per her request. Not that I needed it. I'd never forget a face like hers or who these belonged to.

As I snagged few pics, some random person walking by yelled, "Get a room!" We both laughed. Unfortunately for me, that was the end of the show. She'd quickly tucked herself back into her dress, rewrapping herself in her cardigan and my blazer.

I shoved my phone safely away back into my front pants pocket. "Thank you, Chloe. Really. You did not have to do that."

She shrugged. "I know. I wanted to. Now you'll have something to look at later on down the road, and you can say you've actually *seen* my boobs. Even before Tanner."

Tanner. *Schmuck.* He had no idea what he'd missed out on, for now, anyway. For some selfish and unknown reason, I was hoping he'd never find out. Though, I was sure he'd blow up her phone to get together as soon as her plane touched down. A twinge of an unfamiliar feeling of jealousy seared through me. Unless it was the alcohol kicking in again.

Either way, I needed to get my head together before shit emotionally spiraled any more out of control.

"I, for one, am grateful, but you're telling me he hasn't seen your beautiful boobs yet?"

She shook her head. "Nope. Just a few pics here and there with a lotta cleavage. Ya know, selfies or whatever. And most definitely not in person. We're just barely talking."

*Booya, sucker.*

As comfortable as I'd been just sitting and conversing with Chloe on a very hard, cold bench in a secluded, dark corner, we needed to move to a new, more public location before my hormones had a chance to overtake my brain and I really did bend her over and take advantage of her sweet nature. "Let's move up to that other bench by the sidewalk. I don't trust myself around you anymore."

She let out a playful whine. "Do we have to?"

I stood up and held my hand out to her. "No, we don't *have* to, but I need to."

She reluctantly put her hand in mine, and I pulled her to stand. "Fine. I'll go. But there had better be a good reason for moving."

*Oh, you have no idea what you're in for.*

We gathered up what few things we had and moved out of the darkness and into the glow of street and neon lights.

I wrapped my arm around her shoulders as we sat down. "Looks like whoever said to get a room wasn't talking to us."

She cocked her head to look up at me. "What makes you say that?"

I nodded over my shoulder towards the dark corner where we'd been sitting. "You really can't see shit back there. About the only thing anyone maybe could have seen was our feet."

"What do you mean maybe could have seen? You didn't know we wouldn't be?"

"I mean, I was relatively confident. Just turns out I was right."

"Ohmigod."

"Don't worry, as long as you're with me, I won't put you in a position to be shared."

"Well, that's reassuring." She nestled herself under my arm. "So, we came up here for nothing?"

"Hah. No, not for nothing. I can still see and touch you up here. Maybe just not as much," I said, caressing the back of her neck with my thumb while playing with her hair.

We sat for a while in comfortable silence, watching the world pass by. I'd been watching this tiny pink church just across the street and down a little ways from us. People had been going into and out of it at record speed the entire time we'd been sitting there. "Wonder what's up with that church? Why are so many people getting married in the middle of the night?" Not that I'd truly cared, but it was fascinating.

"Huh?"

I pointed to the chapel. She shifted slightly to face the little church. As she did, the hem of her already short-ass dress rose, stopping just barely below the top of her upper thigh. *Fuck my life*. If that dress climbed any higher, I'd be able to see her panties. The thought brought me back to her sitting cross-legged in front of me at the pool when she'd caught a beachball to the head and, thank the dirty-minded gods above, I'd caught a tiny glimpse of a lip-slip. *Boing. Down, boy!*

I cleared my throat while making my best attempt at inconspicuously adjusting myself.

Chill bumps spread across her bare legs as she watched the church and I eye-fucked her. "Interesting," she said, interrupting my pornographic fantasies of her in various compromising positions. "Maybe they're running a two-for-one special? Buy a marriage, get a free divorce. I'm sure that comes in handy around here."

"It wouldn't surprise me. This is Vegas, after all. Pretty much anything goes. Hell, even I might be on board with something like that. A buy-one, get-one special. Helps keep things less complicated." As much as I'd preferred the less complicated route of a one night stand, mixed with my aversion towards long-term relationships, I'd admired those people—the ones bold enough to throw caution to the wind and elope—the way they walked into that little chapel so confident in their decision to dedicate themselves to each other for the rest of their lives…or the rest of the night. Just walk in, like, fuck it, let's do this.

Or maybe they were just too drunk off their assess to even know the difference. Who was I to judge either way?

I could feel Choe practically burning holes in my head with her stare. "You think you'll ever do it again?"

"Do what again?" Get a taste of you? *Can't fucking wait.*

"Get married."

Okay, sooo not what I'd expected her to say. "Again? I was never married a first time. It was a close call though."

She slapped my thigh, causing my dick to jump—either to get out of the way or as a reaction to her touch, wanting more. Who knew anymore with that thing? As of late, it had a mind of its own.

I grabbed her hand to stop her from pulling it away and held on to it.

We both stared down at our hands locked together.

74

## Lyndsay Marie

"You know what I meant, silly. I'm feeling pretty damned good, so I might not make sense, but I know what I mean. You should too. You said it was a long time ago. Do you think you'll ever want to settle down again or even *get* married, eventually?"

I shrugged. "Haven't really thought much about it, to be honest. I pretty much keep myself busy with work, guys trips, nightly outings. You know, dude stuff." That was the God's honest truth. Yes, I had did what I had to do to have my needs met every few days or so, but I also worked hard, and a hell of a lot more than I got laid. When I wasn't doing either of those, I was networking and socializing.

"And getting your other needs met too, apparently...player".

"Well, yeah, that too. I mean, don't you?" A sly grin spread across her face. *Yeah, that's what I thought.*

While she thought about what I'd said, a bachelorette party paraded past us. It was kind of cute and annoying at the same time—a bunch of drunk women laughing and carrying on, drinking from tall penis-shaped cups, wearing matching shirts and blinking, light-up jewelry. The bride-to-be wore a wedding veil with a bunch of condoms pinned to it.

I had no clue how in the hell I'd gone from scoping out a woman to take to bed one minute to suddenly feeling a little empty, like something was missing in my life...even feeling a little guilty for not being remotely close to walking down the aisle anytime soon—or someone to do it with. Not that I'd had a reason to hurry, because my biological clock wasn't

75

ticking, but without even trying, Chloe had me second-guessing a lot of shit.

"But to answer your question," I continued, pulling myself out of my feels, "I'm sure if the right girl comes along, I'm not opposed to putting a ring on it. What about you? Would you reconsider it, or did your d-bag ex ruin it for you?"

She squeezed my hand. "Hmm. Not really. Maybe. I don't know. It hasn't been that long since Derrick and I broke up. I mean, long enough for me to move on, I think. But not long enough to consider going down that road anytime soon."

"That's a shame, Chloe. I get what you're saying, though, but something tells me you'd make some lucky man really happy in life." Even if it ended up being this Tanner guy.

I didn't know why I had such a strong aversion toward him. I didn't even know him. Hell, I barely knew Chloe. But talking to her was easy and comfortable. Regardless of how many hours we'd known each other, it'd felt like I'd known her for half my life.

Plus, she tasted sweet, like a cookie I'd only gotten a small bite of, and I wanted to devour the whole thing.

Her hand trembled inside of mine, and I wasn't convinced it was from the cold.

"I have another question for you."

"Sure," she said. "Fire away."

"Entertain me for a minute. You said you've never turned down a challenge. So what's the craziest one you've ever taken on?"

# Lyndsay Marie

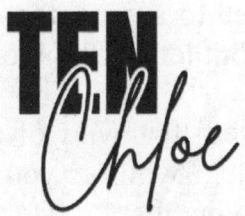

# TEN
## Chloe

In all my years on earth, I'd done a lot of stupid shit. Some things were to be expected for my age at the time…others not so much.

As a kid, I'd played a lot of ding-dong-ditch and egged a few houses. When the teenaged years rolled around, I did some crazier stuff involving bottle rockets, potatoes, and police cars—I'd never tell anyone any more than that.

In college, I'd mellowed out some, but also switched gears. I went from reckless in the streets to reckless in the sheets, which meant Dan and I had a lot more in common than he knew.

The shenanigans didn't stop just because I'd become an adult. I once kissed a stranger on a dare while out at karaoke one night. We'd ended up dating for a few years before he dumped me publicly with a literal mic drop.

You'd think I'd learned my lesson early on in life after being escorted home by the cops a few times that I had nothing to prove, or gain, by not taking on a dare.

So when Dan asked me what the craziest challenge was I've ever taken on, I had to think about which way I wanted to answer that. "Hmm. I've got a few ideas in mind but let me think on it and get back to you."

"You've lived that wild of a life, huh? That's interesting. Well, while you think of an answer, let's add to that list."

"Wha—?" Ignoring my sort of question, Dan stood and stretched. Forget it. It didn't matter what his plan was, I'd had the pleasure of ogling over this incredible specimen of a man.

I had nothing to lose at this point. Anything with him would have been a win-win. He very well could have led me into the sewer with a red balloon, and I would have followed him.

But he'd piqued my curiosity. "Now what are we doing? Are we going somewhere? Because I'm perfectly content sitting right here."

He smiled and my insides liquified, matching my brain. What the hell was he doing to me?

All I'd wanted since being left to my own devices was to get laid. Then Dan had pulled that *I kinda really like you* shit and changed everything.

"You look so damned sexy in my jacket, you know that?"

I looked down at his oversized coat wrapped around my tiny body. "Thank you. And thanks for letting me wear it. It's warm, and it smells amazing too."

"You're most welcome. If your legs get cold, I have some pants you can wear. They might be a little big on you."

I busted out laughing. "You'd take the pants right off your ass for me? Who said chivalry is dead? Now, Dan, what are we doing?"

"I have an idea that might just make it to the top of your list."

This man really thought he was about to get me to do something so insane that it'd top my list? Ha! "I'm listening."

"Have you ever crashed a wedding?"

"Do *what*? You can't be serious." My eyes darted between Dan and the church. *No way.* Did he really...? Holy—. "Are you for real?"

"Hell yeah I am. Come on, let's go."

Okay, now I was really fucking nervous about what he had up his sleeve. Was he serious about crashing a wedding? An actual wedding? Where happy and in-love people were exchanging vows.

He could not be serious.

Then he knelt in front of me, slipped my shoes back on my feet, and buckled each one tight around my ankle.

Yup, he was dead serious.

While he'd worked on my shoes, I'd succumbed to this crazy idea while I combined our drinks into one cup, securing the lid on tight. "This is crazy. *You* are crazy. I can't believe we're doing this."

"Oh, we're just getting started."

80

A shiver ran through me. *Just getting started*? What else could we possibly do that would surpass crashing a wedding?

"What's wrong, Miss. I Never Turn Down A Good Challenge? You're not nervous, are you? Ready to throw in the towel already?"

*Maybe*. Just slightly, and I had a damned good idea why. It was because I'd let someone else take the lead all night when I was used to being the one in charge of, well, everything.

All things considered, up until this point, the night had gone well. Sometimes it'd even felt like a real first date. A good one at that.

Butterflies bounced around my stomach at the thought of it. "Nope. I'm good. Good as gold. Let's get this party started."

I hopped up and stood next to him, grabbing on to his arm to brace myself, catching my balance while everything spun around me. Okay, so maybe I wasn't quite as ready as I'd thought.

"You okay?"

"Yeah. The drinks are definitely kicking in. But I'm all right, though. I think. We'll find out when we start walking."

He smiled and grabbed me by the hand, leading us across the street toward the little pink church where we'd been watching couples filing into and out of the double front doors for their insta-wedding that probably came with a free annulment.

We stopped at one of those old-timey food carts that was parked on the sidewalk just outside of the church and bought a huge bag of gourmet caramel and white cheddar popcorn, loaded down with roasted peanuts and drizzled with dark chocolate.

What's wedding crashing without a tasty snack?

We snuck inside, carting our paraphernalia—drink and big-ass bag of popcorn—hidden under our arms and slipped past a line of giddy—and probably very drunk—couples waiting to fill out their paperwork to say *I do*.

"I can't believe I let you talk me into this." Well, he didn't exactly have to convince me. Then again, there wasn't much he could have offered that I would have said no to.

He wrapped his arm around me, tucking me into his side and guided me to sit down beside him in one of the white folding chairs at the back of the chapel.

"Relax, Chloe. I was only joking. We're not actually going to crash anyone's wedding."

"Oh. We're not?" That was a relief.

"Not technically, no. We're just here to watch...and maybe talk shit about 'em. I mean, the night's still young, if you want it to be, and according to you, you have no curfew."

It was well after midnight, but I had no idea what time it really was. I had no phone, and there wasn't a single clock in sight. The last one I'd seen was at the ice cream shop a few hours ago. "This is true. I'd like to get *some* sleep, eventually. But for now, I'm all yours."

"Fantastic."

"So, is this your way of resisting taking me to bed?"

He gave me side-eye. "Patience, my dear. I also wanted to get you somewhere out of the cold. You were shivering out there. This seemed like a good enough place as any to go."

"Uh, either of our hotel rooms would have been just fine by me." I slapped my hand over my mouth as soon as the words came out, followed by a hiccup mixed with a burp. *Shit.* How fucking gross. *Note to self: you're done drinking. Now and ever.* Maybe not ever, but for now. Probably.

He patted my leg. "You know, I'm not going to lie, Chloe, that's not a bad idea, taking you back to my suite, in spite of your masculine body functions. But as I said earlier, I'm starting to like *you.* I don't know what it is—well, I do—it's a lot of things, but I'd rather just spend time with you first…for now. We'll get there, eventually."

What could I say? The man wanted to appreciate me before hopefully ripping my panties off with his teeth later. I had no argument. "Okay. Fair enough. Let the show begin." I held my breath, holding down another hiccup I felt building.

We kicked back, snacking on our popcorn, just talking about anything and everything basic, and watched people come and go.

"This popcorn is delicious," I said, scooping up another handful and shoving it in my mouth.

Dan held up the almost empty bag. "Must be. We've almost smashed the entire thing."

He handed me our drink, and I washed down the crumbs of popcorn floating around my mouth. "There a logo or name on it? I wanna see if they have a website or something so I can order some and have it shipped."

He held the bag up in the air and spun it around. "Nope, nothing. Just a standard popcorn logo. We can check with them on the way out."

"Don't let me forget." I sat back, propping my feet up on the chair in front of me, and took in my surroundings.

The chapel was decked out in gaudy décor that was just flat-out awful. It was all flashy, old-school Vegas art, with plush, blood red carpet on the floor and gobs of fake, plastic flowers cascading down the walls and draped on the backs of chairs. Hanging on the wall behind a white lattice arch, draped in even more multi-colored artificial flowers, was a huge pink, light-up neon sign that spelled out the word "Love."

Elton John's "Kiss the Bride" played in the background from speakers that sounded like they were as old as the décor.

Jokingly, I said to Dan, "I wonder if you're supposed to grab a handful of those fake flowers off the wall on the way to the altar and use them as a prop to keep as a souvenir?"

A lady who looked twenty years older than she probably was, sitting a few rows in front of us with a lit cigarette hanging loosely between her lips, turned in her chair to face us and said, "Those are extra."

"Wha—? Oh, sorry. I was just joking." Oops. Didn't think anyone else had heard me.

"Eh. There's lots to joke about in here. Stick around some more, you'll see."

Like I hadn't already seen enough craziness?

"So, when are you two going up there?" She flicked ash onto the floor in front of her. "You've been carrying on back here for a while now."

"What? Oh, we're not...we're just friends," I said, because what the hell else could I say? We'd barely known each other a few hours. I'd hardly even considered us friends, and at the rate we were going, we wouldn't end up as each other's one-night fuck either.

"So, you're not here to tie the knot? Huh."

Dan and I looked at each other and laughed. I spoke up first. "God no," I said, with a little too much emphasis on the *no*. I cleared my throat and pulled myself together. "I mean, no," I said more calmly. "We're not here to get married. Just...observing, taking notes." And entertaining ourselves at everyone else's expense.

Dan put his arm around my shoulders. "Yeah, we're just friends."

She shrugged and lit her next cigarette with the one still burning between her lips. "Suit yourselves."

"What about you? Are you waiting to get married?" I knew damned well the old hag wasn't waiting to get married. She'd been sitting there almost as long as we had and would accidentally burn the place down first at the rate she was going, ultimately preventing anyone else from making any life-altering irresponsible decisions.

"Oh, hell no. Been there, done that. Four times. I work here now. It's my job to clean up and straighten the chairs as people come and go." Then she turned her back, facing forward. Guessed she was done with us.

I looked at Daniel and mouthed *awkward*.

He shook his head.

He'd had his arm around me since we'd sat down. I felt his hand rubbing my arm through his coat sleeve. Each time he'd touched me or put his arm around me, did not go unnoticed. Could have been the alcohol, but I was starting to settle into the idea of not getting laid and just enjoying our time together, which was uncharted territory for me.

Even for as long as Derrick and I had been together, it never felt quite right. Something always felt amiss with him, even up until the time when I'd thought he was going to propose to me. I still would have said *yes* because he was my comfort zone.

Now that we'd been broken up, and even despite my talking to Tanner, I was perfectly content going back to the old me...which was supposed to have started tonight.

Yet, here I sat, next to Dan, wondering if I ever would be a bride one day.

More couples than I could keep up with had gotten married as we sat in the back talking and laughing, mostly at ourselves, but sometimes making jokes about the characters—literally—that made their way through.

One couple had actually showed up dressed as the Joker and Harley Quinn. Then three people—two women and a man—made their way front and center, eventually exchanging vows.

"Three? Can they do that? Is that even legal?"

"Apparently it is. You know anything goes in Vegas." Dan had a devilish grin on his face. "You got something against a threesome?"

"Not at all. But that"—I pointed toward the altar— "isn't exactly the kind of threesome I'm familiar with."

He nudged into me. "Oh, yeah? So you've got experience with them, huh?"

"Just once or twice in college." Maybe more, but I figured I'd said enough to get his wheels turning. "What about you? You ever partake in one?"

He rubbed his chin as if he really had to think hard about if he'd ever had one. "A few but not near as far back as college."

"Boy, you really are getting your needs met, huh?"

"I mean, I participate in threesomes on a regular basis, but…let's save that conversation for another time. You know you still haven't answered my question."

"Which one?"

"The craziest thing you've ever done. Surely your list isn't that extensive that you haven't been able to come up with something by now."

I'd forgotten that he'd even asked me, so I told him the first thing that came to mind in that moment. "Probably that one and only time I went skydiving in the nude. Yup, that's definitely it."

"Naked skydive? Wow. That is honestly not the answer I expected. At all. I thought for sure it would've been the threesome."

"Well, surprise!"

"You are full of surprises, Chloe. But that is most definitely not something I think I'd ever consider. Did it hurt?"

I laughed. "No, not really. It felt weird and I don't think I'll ever do it again, myself. I'm pretty sure some parts of me aren't where they were before I jumped out of the plane. But I can at least say I've done it. And what about you, Dan? What's the craziest thing you've ever done?"

He looked at me and there was something in his eyes. Not like an eyelash or speck of dirt, but a playful twinkle with a hint of mischievousness...something that reeked of trouble.

His wicked grin gave away that he was up to something.

He caught me off guard when he stood up, grabbed me by the hand and pulled me up to my feet, flush against him.

With his arms wrapped around me, he said, "Marry you."


To be continued....keep going.

# ELEVEN
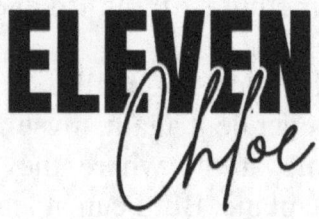
*Chloe*

One Year Later.

What happens in Vegas, stays in Vegas…right?
*Right?*
Wrong.

Oh so very wrong. Especially when I was only supposed to be there for a few days for a girls' trip. That was it. Just me and my two besties having a few drinks, checking out the hotties, enjoying a couple of days away from home. Not doing shit that would potentially haunt me for the rest of my life…like marrying a total stranger. Because that was what happened when I'd allowed myself to get way too distracted by mystery man's ridiculously handsome looks and swoon-worthy personality, not to mention we were both so drunk off our asses that neither one of us thought to swap contact information when all was said and done.

I'm talking nothing.

No last name, no idea where he'd lived beyond the state of Illinois, not even a single digit from a phone number. All I was left with was as much of his first name as he was willing to give me—because I didn't want to assume that Dan was even his first or real name—the image of the way his ass looked in custom-fitted dress pants, and his reassurance that we'd take care of it all on Monday. Oh, and his high-dollar sport coat.

Face. Meet. Palm.

Because that was the kind of shit that followed me home and did not stay in Vegas.

It'd been well over a year since our trip. Sometimes I'd thought about going back to that little pink church with the blood-red carpet and tacky artificial plastic flowers of every color, just to look through the guest registry and confirm for myself that it had in fact happened and it wasn't all just a dream...or for some, a horror show.

"You're awfully quiet over there. You okay?" Katie asked, breaking me out of my trance down memory lane.

I took a sip of my drink. "I'm good. Great. Just fine."

She eyed me suspiciously. "Really? Because you don't sound fine."

"Well, I am. I think I'm just ready to get off this god-forsaken plane and see Rowan. I really miss her. That's all. We haven't seen her in person since she moved away." Okay, so I wasn't *fine*, because I truly did miss my BFF. But everything else felt off-kilter, and I couldn't put my finger on why all of a sudden out of nowhere my shotgun marriage had decided to come to the forefront of my brain now. I'd like to think it was all this wedding stuff stirring up memories I didn't want to relive.

"Something is up with you. Not only have you not been your overly talkative, goofy self, but you've been working on that same drink for the entire flight." She pointed to my cup, then folded her arms across her chest as she relaxed back into her seat. "It's usually you who's the one encouraging the bad behavior." After a few seconds of silence, she shot upright and smacked my arm causing me to almost drop my damn cup. "Ohmigod. You're pregnant? Aren't you?"

I felt my face twist into a confounded look. "What the fuck, Kat?" I practically yelled. The lady across the aisle glared over at us. I lowered my volume to a frustrated whisper. "No! Jesus. I am not pregnant. Jesus. That would require sex…with a man or some magical, sperm-producing battery-operated boyfriend. Not just me, myself, and I." Lord knew there hadn't been a lot of *that* going on as of late since I'd called things off with Tanner a while back. "Why would you even—never mind. I told you, I'm fine."

"If you say so. But I'll find out. I always do." She leaned back again, closing her eyes, seemingly content with my answer for now. "I'll have to agree with you on one thing, though—I miss Rowan too. I still can't believe she's getting married."

"Hell, I can't believe she and Wes have waited this long to do it. I had my money on them eloping less than six months after they met."

"Not me. Rowan's too level-headed for that. Not to mention everything she went through with David. Even a good dick wouldn't cloud her judgment into doing some dumb shit like get married on a whim."

I rolled my eyes and looked back out the window as the clouds quickly floated by. "Eh. I think when you know, you know. You know? You can't put a timeline on love. If she'd have married him after six hours or six years of knowing him, I'd have supported her either way."

"I would too. I'm just saying, I think she did right by waiting at least this long. And six hours? That seems a touch extreme."

Ha! Little did she know that I'd done just that— because even after all this time I'd yet to confess to any of my close and best friends about my own shotgun wedding. Literally. I'd married a man after only knowing him for less than twelve hours. More than six, but way less than what most would have considered socially acceptable. "It was an exaggeration, Kat. Chill."

The stewardess approached with a trash bag, and I tossed my mostly full cup of warm, watered-down screwdriver into it. What a waste. I didn't recall a time I'd ever thrown out that much of a mixed drink.

Plus, I'd had enough on my mind to even worry about dumping out a free drink with cheap booze. All catching a buzz did to me anymore was have me thinking about *him*—Dan—and our brief time together, which seemed like a lifetime ago. I couldn't help but wonder if I crossed his mind as much as he did mine, if ever.

Thankfully, Kat didn't give me any more shit for the rest of the flight. The plane finally landed, and we filed off the plane, making our way to the baggage claim. Kat grabbed my arm as we walked. "What the—? I just got a text from Rowan. Looks like she's sending someone else to pick us up."

"You serious? Why? I was really looking forward to seeing her first." I stuck out my bottom lip and pouted. "Who's picking us up, then?"

"I don't know why or who. All her text says is: Sorry, can't make it. Sending back up. Y'all will know when you see. Love you, see y'all soon."

"We'll know? Well, what kinda shit is that?"

"No clue. Guess we'll find out soon enough."

We grabbed our luggage off the carousel and headed outside to the curbside pickup zone. I sat down on top of one of my two over-sized suitcases and sent Rowan a text of my own.

Kat scanned the sea of cars and SUVs parked along the curb. "This is ridiculous. How are we supposed to *know* when we see. See what?"

"Yeah, I got nothing. I just sent her a text asking her what the hell she was up to, and her response was a bunch of laughing-crying smiley faces. Glad she thinks this shit is funny." I glanced around but didn't see anything obvious or out of the ordinary either. So I put my attention back on my phone.

A few minutes later, Kat busted out laughing and smacked my arm. "Oh. My. God. Chlo. You are not going to believe this."

I looked up from my phone, my gaze following the direction she was pointing, and almost tipped over.

Standing a short distance down from us, seemingly lost in a group of tourists waiting in the bus loading zone, was a man with his back to us, apprehensively holding up a neon green poster board with bold, black letters that read "Waiting for My Two Favorite Hookers."

Lyndsay Marie

"No she didn't." *Oh, Rowan, payback is gonna be a bitch*. The wheels turned as I thought of how I was going to reword my entire bridesmaid toast.

"Looks like she did." Kat rounded up her luggage and started to make her way over to the man with the sign. "Hey!" she called out to him.

It was all fun and games until he turned around.

Because that wasn't just any man.

It was *him*.

Dan.

From Vegas.

The man whose face was the last thing I'd seen before I closed my eyes at night, the first thing I pictured when I woke up each morning and practically every waking moment in between. Also, whose scent had been permanently etched into the deepest part of my memory. Never mind the fact I could still smell his scent on the sport coat hanging in my closet. The same man who the last time I saw him, we'd just gotten married ourselves.

Now here he was, standing less than fifty feet from me.

Kat waved at him as he turned, grabbing his attention. She glanced back at me over her shoulder as she approached him. "Come on, Chloe. This is obviously our ride."

I held my breath as I stood up.

*Shit.*

Dan's face turned a bright shade of red. I didn't know if it was from embarrassment from holding up that ridiculous sign, or from mortification as recognition hit him like a ton of bricks as soon as we locked eyes. My guess was both. Because I felt every single emotion that was clearly etched all over his face.

Seeing him again after all this time, every feeling I'd felt for him but adamantly denied since we'd met, came back with a raging vengeance. Except now they were mixed with a whole lot of awkwardness and what-the-fucks because *how in the hell did we get here?*

# TWELVE

Awkward: an adjective used to describe a lack of having grace or causing embarrassment or something along those lines, according to the dictionary.

Unfortunate as it was, I could relate to that word on every level at various points in my life, and on more than one occasion. Looking back, two very specific moments stood out more than others.

The first incident was that time in junior high when I'd gotten caught red-handed by my girlfriend's dad, making out and getting handsy with his little princess on his front porch after a homecoming dance. The second being that screwed-up time during residency when I was assisting in a major surgery and thought I had to fart but shit my pants instead. That was all it took for me to become the laughingstock of the OR for a long time. But I did quit talking trash about staff who had to wear those ugly, blue paper scrubs for being careless after that.

And that latter incident had a strong probability of occurring a second time. Except I wasn't in a surgery. I was standing in a crush of people at the airport.

*Fuck.*

Who would have guessed just how awkward, mixed with a heaping scoop of unpleasant and uncomfortable, it would be to end up face-to-face with the woman I'd challenged to marry me on a whim without even having known her last name. Then I'd unwillingly ghosted her.

Now here I stood, holding up the brightest neon fucking green sign known to man, insinuating she was a hooker—on both sides of the cardboard because Rowan insisted on a two-sided poster.

Because that's exactly what'd happened when I'd been volunteered to pick up Wes's fiancé's two best friends from the airport. I had no idea who the hell I was even supposed to be looking for, since Rowan refused to show me any pictures. She just gave me this big-ass sign to hold up for all of Chicago O'Hare to bear witness to, and a time to be in the pick-up zone, along with the reassurance they'd find me right away. I'd never been more confused in my life.

Boy, they found me all right.

The English language didn't have enough expletive sentence enhancers for neither the shitshow of a situation Rowan had unknowingly put me in, nor for the foreign feelings that'd resurfaced from out of nowhere. Ones that I was sure I'd long locked up tight the moment I left Vegas.

As I stood front and center, surrounded by strangers from all over the globe, my ego shrinking by the minute, a very tall, poised woman with perfectly placed, bleach-blonde hair walked straight up to me, like she knew right away I was who she was looking for.

She pointed to the sign, now dangling loosely by my side as every fiber of my being deflated. "This looks like a Rowan move."

I forced a smile as best I could, as my grip tightened on the poster. "Indeed it is."

"Katie." She offered her hand to me. "It's nice to meet you...sorry, I don't know your name. Rowan didn't tell us who was picking us up. She just said we'd know."

*Katie.* I'd heard her name mentioned a few times here and there, but I'd never seen her in pictures. I never cared enough to ask. She was absolutely stunning, though—like a Victoria's Secret supermodel. As angelic as she was, she paled in comparison to the beautiful creature just behind her in the distance. The one that, all this time later, even after zero contact, apparently still did things for me...inside and out.

I glanced at Chloe, again, who'd finally slowly started making her way over to us, her stare drilling into me.

"Dan—." I cleared my throat and shook Katie's hand. "I'm Daniel."

Katie was all smiles and giddiness, half bouncing out of her shoes with excitement. It was kind of cute, kind of annoying. "It's nice to finally meet you, Daniel, and put a face to a name."

"Same to you."

"We've heard a lot about y'all up here."

*Great.* Couldn't wait to find out just how much more Chloe had learned about me. "I bet. Here, let me get those for you." I took her suitcases and wheeled them around the back of my car. I tossed the poster into the trunk first, then set her luggage on top of it.

Chloe had finally made her way over and stood beside my car, watching my every move and waiting for who knew what. All I knew was she made me nervous as hell. I inched closer to her, carefully grabbed the smallest suitcase from her grip and stacked it in the trunk next to Katie's. "Trunk's full," I said, slamming the lid closed. "I'll have to stick that other one in the backseat with you. I'd offer you front seat, but, um, looks like your friend already claimed shotgun."

She cut her eyes to Katie, then back to me. "She always does."

I turned my hand palm side up, raising it just enough for her to see my olive branch, of sorts. It was the best I could do in a crunch. "I'm Daniel, by the way." If nothing else, I at least wanted to be cordial with her. She didn't take my hand or offer her own in return.

"So I heard."

Well, we were off to a fantastic start. Rejected handshake, pointed answers. She was pissed, or at least it'd seemed that way. The next two weeks were going to be interesting.

Couldn't. Fucking. Wait.

It dawned on me that, as Chloe gave me the evil eye, she had only ever known me as Dan. When I'd introduced myself to her for the first time, it was only ever with the intent of getting laid. Full names, middle names, last names didn't matter. Even as we'd said "I do," we'd chosen to only go by the names we'd already known each other as—Dan and Chloe. Without having talked to her since then, I could only assume that was just the beginning of what exposing information was yet to come.

I rubbed the back of my neck. Every muscle in my body ached with tension.

"Listen, I—."

"It's fine." She cut me off mid-sentence. "We can talk later. If we keep standing here in this weird stand-off too much longer, Sherlock Holmes up there is gonna get even more suspicious of me, and probably you too."

Just as she'd said the words, Katie rolled her window down and leaned out. "What is taking y'all so long? Can we please get going? I wanna see Rowe!" Then she slinked back inside the car and the window went up.

"Boy, she doesn't miss much," I said out loud, more to myself as a mental note for future reference.

I took Chloe's other suitcase, shoving it into the backseat, then gestured for her to climb inside.

"Told you," she said with a sarcastic smirk.

I threw my hands up in surrender. *Easy, girl.* "I never said a word."

As she moved past me, I caught a whiff of her scent—the same one I remembered very vividly from before. It hadn't changed. In fact, nothing about her seemed to have changed. She still had the same hazel-green eyes, wavy, dark auburn hair that somehow glimmered under fluorescent lighting, and big, bouncy boobs.

Right before she ducked in, she paused, looking me dead at me. "Name's still Chloe, just in case you were wondering, *Daniel.*"

*Ouch.*

Then she winked and closed the door.

Christ. If I ever wanted to know the definition of mixed signals, all I had to do was look her up.

Lyndsay Marie

Her physical traits and scent might not have changed, but she had a whole lot of sass that was new to me. Truth be told, I kinda liked 'em a little feisty.

*Challenge accepted.*

I wedged myself behind the wheel of my car, thankful to finally be on the move. We'd almost made it to the interstate before Katie broke the heavy silence that filled my car. "Thanks for picking us up. Any idea why Rowan didn't do it herself?"

"From what I know, she and Wes had a meeting with the building tenant about securing the rooftop for the wedding or something. She didn't go into a whole lot of detail, and to be honest, I lost interest in what she was saying when she handed me that sign."

"Ah. I figured it was wedding related. I cannot believe she sent you with that ridiculous thing. I mean, I can, but wow. How'd she get you to agree to go along with her shenanigans?"

Ridiculous was an understatement. "Trust me. The last thing I wanted was to hold it up for everyone at O'Hare to see. Initially Wes threatened to remove me from the wedding party if I didn't do it. Even though I knew he wouldn't. It wasn't until Rowan threatened to kick my ass. And judging from her moodiness as of late, it wasn't worth the risk."

"That sounds about right."

"Yeah, and she refused to tell me anything about who I was picking up. I didn't exactly have a choice but to hold it up. I guess that was all part of her master plan."

"Who knows anymore with her. She can be a real mean-ass when she wants to, but I've never known her to actually hurt a fly." Katie practically turned all the way around to Chloe in the back seat. "You're awfully quiet back there."

When Chloe responded, her voice barely reached to the front cab of the car. "Guess I don't have a lot to say."

"How are you not as excited as me to be here and finally see Rowan? You've barely said a word since we left Memphis."

"I already told you once, I am excited."

"Well, you don't act excited. You're off the plane now. So there's that excuse. What else you got?"

"Just got a lot on my mind. That's all."

"Okay, well, pull that stick out of your ass." Katie looked at me. "Excuse my friend here. She's apparently going through a life crisis or some shit."

I knew exactly what Chloe was going through, at least in the last twenty minutes or so, and it wasn't some life crisis. Well, maybe it was to her. "No worries. I get that way sometimes around new people. I'm sure it's nothing a glass of pink champagne or shot of top-shelf Patrón can't take care of." I snuck a peek in the rearview mirror at Chloe. She stared out the window, her elbow propped up on the door, hand over her mouth. She cut her eyes at me for a split second and tried her damnedest to hide a smile.

*Yeah, I'm onto you and your game.*

"Ain't that the truth," Katie said. "Actually, a shot sounds like a really good idea, except that one back there"—she pointed to Chloe—"apparently doesn't seem to want to drink much anymore."

I didn't look this time, but I could sense Chloe rolling her eyes. "Huh, is that so? Well, there's nothing wrong with that. But we might have to convince her to change her mind."

"Good luck with that. She's damned hardheaded. Anyway, enough about Debbie Downer—how far are we from Rowan's? I could really use that drink."

Katie had no idea just how much I agreed with her. "Hmm. We're not too far. Traffic is light, so maybe less than ten minutes? I'm not a hundred percent sure they'll have Patrón, specifically. But I don't live far from them. If you want, I can drop you guys off and run over to my place and grab a bottle if that's your drink of choice. I know for a fact I have it." I'd had the same bottle sitting in my liquor cabinet, unopened since I was in Vegas. I'd bought it on my way to the airport as sort of a souvenir.

Now, by the grace of God, act of good Karma, and all the stars aligning, I had the one and only souvenir from Las Vegas I'd ever need sitting in the back seat of my car.

# THIRTEEN

*Chloe*

My life could be summed up in three words: what, the, and fuck. I never thought I'd see Dan, well, Daniel, ever again. Not because I didn't want to, but given our circumstances when we'd met and the way he'd left me, reuniting with him seemed damned near impossible...or so I'd thought.

The last time we saw each other, we'd just gotten married. *Married!*

The beginning of the end of our time together started out with one hell of a superhot make-out session—the one I'd waited on bated breath for all night long—that'd kicked-off as soon as we went barreling through the exit doors of that little pink wedding chapel. It continued all the way down the street, into the elevator lobby at the Bellagio.

Our celebration was cut short when Daniel was interrupted by a string of phone calls and texts from one of his friends, which had turned out to be an emergency and he'd needed to go. He said he would be in touch. Then he turned and jogged away before either one of us had realized we didn't get to swap contact information. I was left standing alone, confused, and hornier than I'd ever been in my entire life.

After he took off, I hung out in the main lobby for a while until I dozed off on a sofa by the elevators and a bellhop woke me up. Confused and with a pounding head, I dragged ass back to the suite. Rowan and Kat were passed out in their king-sized bed, probably long before I'd ever thought of how their night had gone.

When I'd finally woken from the dead, Kat and I talked over a cup of coffee. It wasn't until then that I'd found out how their night had really gone. She caught me up on everything she'd known, which was bits and pieces from what Rowan had told her. I felt like a shitty friend for not being there, but I had no way of knowing about what had happened with them; I didn't have my phone on me the entire night. They did the race together, and they'd made it back to our suite long before me.

Once Kat had finished telling me about their night, she asked me about the rest of mine. My first thought was how much fun I'd had, most of it still a drunken blur. But the memory of how Dan had made me feel was very real and very present—then and now.

The way each one of his touches had sent shock waves of lust through me, his brilliant smile that could light up an entire room and liquefied my insides. Or how we'd gotten married.

Panic set in as she and I talked.

I got *married*? I looked down at my left hand. No ring. That was a relief. But I had to find him. It was later in the morning than I would have preferred, but I'd hoped it was still early enough I still had time to find him because I had no idea where his room was or when his flight was leaving.

So, I gave her a sugar-coated story about hanging out by the pool until it had finally closed, then I lied and told her I'd gone back to the karaoke bar for a few drinks by myself with no luck of getting laid. She didn't ask what time I made it in, and I didn't offer her the information.

When I was done telling her about my night, I gave her quick a hug and told her I loved her and I was going back to the pool if she needed me.

Eventually she and Rowan did make their way down to the indoor pool, but only to tell me that they were going to the hospital to see the man whose life Rowan had saved. I declined their offer to go because my hope was Dan would still show up. He never did.

Now, seeing Daniel again all this time later, every one of those feelings I'd felt then—those in-the-moment feelings—were back with a vengeance.

Who would have guessed it? The one time I'd taken someone up on a dare—*because I am not one to turn down a good challenge*—I did the craziest, and quite possibly the stupidest thing I could have ever done in my lifetime. And out of all the people to have done it with, I find out he's in my best friend's wedding. Literally one of the groom's best friends. I had no idea anytime Rowan mentioned Wesley's friend Daniel she was talking about Dan. *My* Dan.

The. Entire. Time.

As the pieces started falling together and I'd learned it was him, I wanted to scream and rip every strand of hair on my head out by the root. How would I have known? There's no way I could have. I didn't think to ask her to send me pictures of who she was talking about, and she didn't offer. It wasn't important. All I knew was he was a friend of Wesley and Warren's, and now hers.

My one saving grace in this massive clusterfuck of epic proportions was knowing Daniel and I were never legally married.

Yup, that's right. It was all just for show. Seemed like we were told that as we signed paperwork to walk down the aisle, but neither of us, more specifically me, had paid attention to that one minor detail. I could only assume he knew too, after all this time, since he was the one who was supposed to *take care of things* whenever he got home. How in the hell I thought or trusted that he was going to do that on his own was beyond me.

I blamed those sexy shots of top-shelf Patrón we'd taken.

Eventually, after a few very long months of not hearing a word from him or anyone, for that matter, I'd taken it upon myself to find that little pink church on Google Maps and gave them a call. Their receptionist immediately redirected me to the county courthouse for marriage and divorce records. So, I looked them up, and after spending almost a half hour on the phone with them, getting bounced around from person to person, I ended up back on the phone with the church, who'd then dug through their records and informed me that Daniel's and my wedding was all just for fun. It was one of those extra services they offered—all the experience without the hassle and headache.

Who the hell knew that was even a thing? I sure didn't. But that explained why, when I'd called the courthouse, they had no records of our marriage. Hindsight, I probably could have confided in Rowan or Kat or even Mia, but I'd been so embarrassed for what I did, I still to this day couldn't bring myself to tell them the truth about that night.

One day.

Maybe.

"We're almost there." Daniel's sexy voice broke into my wandering thoughts. *Sexy?* I'd been around that man less than a half an hour and already my brain was trying to disconnect from my heart, thinking with only one organ—and it wasn't in my chest.

Kat was right about one thing—I needed to pull the stick out of my ass. It wasn't anyone's fault but my own for what I'd been through between Vegas and Tanner and now unexpectedly reuniting with my fake ex-husband. But if I didn't get my shit together, Kat and Rowan would eventually drag it all out of me before I was ready to spill the beans.

"I'm so excited." Kat bounced in her seat in front of me. "Thank you again for picking us up. Sorry you had to hold up that stupid sign."

Daniel smiled. It was just as I remembered. That panty-burning, blinging-white-toothed, dimple-showing smile. I sighed and wondered if he'd thought of me as much as I did him.

"It was nothing," he said. "If either of you needs anything while you're in town, just let me know. I'm more than happy to help since Wes and Rowan are going to be busy."

*If he only knew the things I'd ask him to help me with.*

112

A few minutes later we were in downtown Chicago, parked in an underground parking garage. We unloaded Daniel's car and stuffed ourselves in an elevator. The car ride here wasn't nearly as uneasy as the one on the elevator. What could have been one of those sexy scenarios in a steamy romance book where the guy takes the girl against the wall and makes dirty promises to her, turned out to be crammed, hotter than necessary—and not in a good way—and Daniel was nowhere near in a position to pin me up against a wall.

We barely stepped foot into the hallway when Rowan came flying out of nowhere, practically tackling me and Katie to the ground. My mood instantly lifted. Turned out I just needed my best friend.

"Ohmigod! Y'all are finally here!" she squealed, wrapping her arms around us. Katie jumped and screamed. Rowan bounced and laughed. I was sandwiched between them, being shook back and forth, my ears ringing from the high-pitched noises coming out of both of their mouths.

"Okay, okay," I said, wiggling my way out. "Easy on the girls. Y'all can't just go squishing me up like that. You'll hurt something."

Rowan stood back and reached forward with both hands and gave my boobs a lift. "I've missed you, and these,'" she said, grabbing her own boobs. "Can't wait for mine to be that big one day."

I heard a moan from somewhere behind Rowan, who I assumed was Wesley. "They're just fine the way they are."

Rowan rolled her eyes. "Come inside. We have lots to talk about and catch up on." She led us into her condo, Wesley and Daniel following behind us with Kat's and my luggage in tow.

We piled into their condo. "Y'all feel free to make yourselves at home," Rowan said. "I'm gonna grab some drinks. Wesley, will y'all put their stuff in the guest room?"

He bowed dramatically then carted our stuff away, disappearing down a hallway.

"Rowan, y'all's place is gorgeous!" Kat said, making her way to the massive open living room.

I followed behind her and plopped down on the huge sectional.

Rowan joined us with an arm full of bottled water. We each took one. "Thank you. I'm so damn happy y'all are here and can finally see it."

"Are you ladies hungry?" Wesley asked, entering the room. "Or should I say, I hope you're hungry. I'm making lasagna for dinner here shortly."

"I could eat," Kat said.

"Me too, for sure. Especially if I'm not the one cooking it."

Wesley wrapped his arms around Rowan and planted a kiss on her temple. They were ridiculously cute, and borderline disgustingly happy. I couldn't even be mad at her. She deserved happiness after everything she'd been through. Hell, we all did, but I was glad to see her in such a good place.

"I'm so sorry, y'all. I didn't do formal or reintroductions. Y'all already know Wesley." We'd met him once when he'd showed up in Memphis to get Rowan to move with him. "And you met Daniel on the way here."

Daniel half-ass waved to everyone in the room, his gaze pointed directly at me. He cleared his throat. "Hi, everyone."

"Hey," Kat and I said in unison. It took everything in my power not to stare at him. Just his presence had a way of drawing me in.

"Gotta watch out for this one," Rowan said, turning toward Daniel. And I couldn't agree more with her statement. "Are you gonna stick around for dinner? You know we'll have plenty."

He shoved his hands in his pockets, standing front and center of the room, looking uncomfortable having been called out. "I'm not entirely sure yet. I need to get with Warren and see if he still wants to get together later."

Rowan rolled her eyes. "Typical. Well, he's supposed to stop by in a bit. Maybe y'all can cancel your Friday night plans for a change and hang out with us?"

He shrugged. "Guess we'll have to wait and see."

# FOURTEEN

*Chloe*

Thankfully, the rest of the afternoon had gone by without a hitch. I'd managed to get a few minutes to myself, away from the chaos, to take a shower and change into what Rowan called my "socially acceptable" pajamas including a bra, per her request, before rejoining everyone back in the kitchen / living area.

I took a seat at the bar next to Katie, who was picking apart a piece of garlic bread. "It smells amazing in here."

Wesley stood at the stove mixing something in a pot, as steam billowed around him. "Thank you," he said over his shoulder. "It's a family recipe. Shouldn't be too much longer; it'll all be ready. Help yourself to some garlic bread."

Watching him, I knew exactly why Rowan had just packed up her life and moved across the country. I probably would have too.

I swiped a chunk of bread off the plate in front of Katie. "So, Rowan, what's the game plan for the next two weeks? I know you have a spreadsheet somewhere with every day plotted out from now until the end of the wedding."

"Ugh, actually, I don't. Well, I did, but I can't find it. I have some ideas and I think I've just about got everything picked out that we're gonna need. I just need y'all with me to make sure everything looks good together."

"Pushing it to the last minute? That doesn't sound like you," Kat said. "Both of y'all have been out of character lately. Is there something going on here that I don't know about?"

Rowan and I looked at each other and said, "Nope."

The doorbell rang, and it sounded like everyone in the entire room yelled, "Come in," at the same time. I swung around in the barstool to see who it was, not that I'd even recognize anyone.

As the door opened, a very tall, handsome man walked in, with another fine piece of ass following right behind him.

The words "holy shit" slipped out of my mouth and a hand smacked my arm.

"Shut your filthy mouth," Katie said under her breath.

Hell, I couldn't help it. I'd never seen a better-looking group of men all in the same room before.

Rowan ran up to the first man and gave him a hug, introducing him to us as her future brother-in-law.

*Ooooh...that's him*? Wowza. I mean, she did say he was a hunk, but I wasn't ready for *that*. And the more I looked at him, the more I saw the resemblance between him and his brother.

Wesley rounded the bar and grabbed and hugged the second man. "Shane, what the hell are you doing here? I thought you said—."

"Yeah, I know what I said. Change of plans."

Rowan hugged Shane next and introduced herself. "Nice to finally meet you in person." She looked around then introduced Shane to me and Kat as Wesley and Warren's childhood best friend. "This is a huge surprise for all of us."

"Yeah, tell me about it," Warren said. "He was in the elevator when I got on to come up here. Surprised the hell out of me."

Warren shook my hand as we said our hellos, then moved on to Katie, and good lawd, she was all red-faced and heart-eyes when he moved his attention to her.

While the other guys caught up and did their hugging and handshaking, Rowan broke up Warren and Katie's little moment. "Warren, Shane, y'all come in, sit, get comfy. I know Kat and Chloe have had a long day. I imagine you have too." Then she called out for Wesley to fix everyone a glass of wine. So much for the tequila.

Warren moved around the kitchen, pulled out a few long-stem glasses, and lined them up on the counter, filling each one a little more than half full. I knew then he was going to make Rowan a really good husband. He could cook and knew how to fill up a wine glass.

Kat grabbed two glasses and slid one over to me. "Drink, bitch."

I picked up the glass and took a hefty gulp. "Wow, that burns. But I needed it. Thank you, Wesley."

"Anytime." He turned his back to the room and put his attention back on the food in front of him.

I stuck my tongue out at Kat. "See," I whispered. "Not pregnant."

She clinked her glass to mine. "Cheers to that."

It'd been a long day and I was exhausted. All I wanted to do was enjoy my little glass of wine, maybe consider a second one, smash through a gluttonous amount of Wesley's homemade lasagna and garlic bread, then call it a night. I knew Rowan had the next two weeks crammed full of wedding planning and finalizing, so there wouldn't be much resting going forward.

I took a few sips from my glass and caught a glimpse of Daniel over my shoulder. He'd made his way to the couch and was now sitting comfortably next to Warren, who was chatting it up with Shane. All of them had quickly made themselves at home on the sectional with their feet propped up on the coffee table. It was exactly the life I'd envisioned for myself. One day.

Rowan grabbed the other three glasses of red wine, made her way into the living room, and offered them to the guys.

Kat turned toward Rowan. "And what's with you, Row? Where's your wine? Are you not drinking?"

"Um. No, not tonight."

"Good grief. Since when did both of y'all quit drinking?" Kat rolled her eyes to me.

I shrugged.

"Y'all realize you're both the reason I even drink?"

"Well, I can't," Rowan said. "I'm on antibiotics for a UTI."

"Suuure. Whatever you have to tell yourself. One glass won't kill you."

"So," Wesley asked the guys from the kitchen as he pulled a massive pan of lasagna out of the oven. "What's the plan? Warren? Daniel? Are you two staying for dinner or what? I know Shane is. He never turns down food. There's plenty here for everyone."

"You know me. I'm going to eat," Shane said.

"Ah, I don't know. We haven't talked about it yet." Warren looked at Daniel whose, eyes darted between him and me, from clear across the room. *Don't look at me.* I wanted no part of this.

Before either of them could come up with an answer, the doorbell rang. This time no one yelled for the mystery visitor to enter. Everyone looked at each other.

"I wonder who that is?" Rowan asked, making her way to the door. She checked the peephole. "It's Camilla," she called out, letting in the next guest.

All the guys echoed "hey" and "hi" and "what's up" as Camilla walked in.

Rowan introduced her new friend to me and Katie first. "Y'all, this is Camilla. She's a co-worker and friend of Wesley and Daniel's."

Camilla sauntered over, her ass swaying back and forth as she stuck her hand out to shake Katie's hand, then mine. "It's a pleasure to meet you both."

Without ever having to see the look on Katie's face, I was one hundred percent sure she and I both were on the same page about Camilla. Not that either one of us had any reason to feel threatened by her, but holy shit, she was gorgeous. And in a very over-the-top kind of way. She had jet-black hair that hung all the way down to her perfect bubble butt, which was only further accentuated by her skin-tight, gold satin dress. Her figure reminded me of Jessica Rabbit. I could only imagine what was going through the guys minds as she walked by. Compared to her, in my current unkempt state of pajamas with my post-shower hair a complete mess, I felt like lukewarm, dirty dishwater.

"So what brings you around?" Rowan asked her. "I wasn't expecting to see you until next week. I thought you were out of town for work?"

"I was. I came back a bit early." Camilla flung her long, flowy hair over her shoulder. "Wesley said friends would be flying in today. I wanted to go ahead and meet them, say hello."

"Oh, yeah. I didn't know if he'd told you or not when they were coming. Well here they are." Rowan looked Camilla up and down from head to toe. "You're dressed up awfully fancy for the occasion." *Yeah, boy, was she ever.*

"Oh, I'm not staying. Just passing by. You know? Places to go, etcetera. I thought I'd stop in for a minute. Plus, I saw Daniel's car parked in the front of the garage." She looked at him. "Still on for tonight?"

Wesley cleared his throat from somewhere behind me. "So, dinner? Anyone? It's ready."

# FIFTEEN
*Daniel*

I always figured I'd be single forever. Not because I couldn't get a woman. Shit, that was the easy part. I'd learned very early on that all I ever had to do was slap on one of my panty-dropping smiles—one that I'd spent a shit-ton of money on to maintain–toss out the whole *I'm a doctor* line, and *bam*—women were on my dick like flies on shit.

But after that stint with my ex, being single seemed like the appropriate thing to do for myself and for anyone who'd remotely shown interest in me. I knew like hell I wasn't ready for any kind of relationship. But on the other hand, I also knew deep down, beneath my well-kept superficial lifestyle, that I would eventually want to settle down. My problem was, I'd yet to cross paths with anyone who remotely held my interest for the title of being my girlfriend, much less the title of wife.

Until now.

I knew from the beginning that Chloe was different from any other woman I'd met. Not because she said so or had to do anything to convince me of it. I felt it in my bones—not just the one in my pants either. That was a bonus. But I felt right about her with every fiber of my soul, a place where I hadn't felt anything emotional in a long time.

Truth be told, I'd never once thought in a million years Chloe would have agreed to marry me. When I told her to—because, yes, I told her, I didn't ask—it was half joke, half why the hell not? So when she'd said *yes*, I had a split-second decision to make: tell her I was only kidding, that I just wanted to see if she'd actually do it, or dive in head-first. I assured her it could easily be undone with an annulment. I only knew that because of a Google search I'd done when I ran to the bathroom at one point.

Either way it wasn't the smartest thing I'd ever done. But I didn't really give a shit at that point. Challenging her was worth the risk—then and now.

We were just getting started.

\*\*\*

"Yo, Shane." I gave a few knocks on my guest bedroom door. "I'm running down to the coffee shop to grab some breakfast. You wanna go?"

Shane showing up was a pleasant surprise for everyone, myself included. As far as I knew, he hadn't

126

been in town since he'd moved away for a new job. Him showing up without anyone knowing also meant he got the pleasure of staying with me because I was the only one with any space left once Wes and Warren's family and out-of-town friends had arrived.

"Nah," he called out from behind the closed door. "I'm straight here." The door cracked open and he barely stuck his head out. "I'm gonna take a shower, but would you mind grabbing me a large, black coffee and maybe a muffin or something?"

"Yeah, sure. Any particular flavor?"

"Anything but chocolate."

I craned my neck trying to get a peek inside my guest room. Shane stood blocking my view into the bedroom. It was pitch-black, thanks to the black-out curtains, so it didn't matter. I couldn't see shit. "Who you trying to hide in here?" I asked jokingly.

He held his stance firm, pulling the door tighter shut. "Huh? Nobody. I've just made a mess of your room. Don't worry, I'll clean it up after I get out of the shower."

"Umm-hmm. You know I don't give a shit if you brought someone here. I was just screwing with you."

"Cool. Well, thanks for the coffee and shit."

"Yeah, I'll be right back. It's just around the corner."

I left my apartment without further incident, smiling and shaking my head at the thought of Shane bringing someone back to my place. I hadn't known Shane nearly as long as Wesley and Warren had, but for the time I had known him, I'd learned he and I were a lot alike.

I grabbed my keys and wallet and made my way down to the coffee shop. It was one of my favorite places to go. Not only was it convenient but they made their pastries fresh daily and ground their coffee per order. It was almost always packed, no matter the time of day, but worth my time to stand in line for sometimes twenty minutes or longer.

After I'd placed my order, I stood to the side of the room and skimmed through work email on my phone. Scroll, scroll, scroll. Boring, boring, boring. *Could one hospital possibly change their policies anymore in one week?* Once the girl at the counter called my name, I grabbed Shane's and my stuff. As I turned to leave, someone caught my eye and I froze in place.

"Chloe?" I said it like a question, but I knew damned well it was her.

"Dan—Daniel? Hi. Hey. What are you doing here?"

I held up two coffees and a paper bag. "Breakfast. You know I live just right around the corner?"

128

"Oh! Yea." *Of course you don't know that.* How could she? She fidgeted with her bracelet. "Yeah, I mean, no, I didn't know that. Rowan wasn't feeling great this morning, so I told her I'd go grab some stuff for everyone. Plus I needed some fresh air."

"Right. You know you passed like two coffee shops to get here?"

She moved up in the line. "I know. But according to Google this place had better reviews. It was only a few blocks over."

"Gotcha. Hey, do you have time to talk? I promise I won't keep you long."

She looked around, then checked the time on her phone. "Sure. As long as I get back soon. I don't need the girls sending out the cavalry to look for me. They already didn't want me coming here alone."

"Okay. I'll go grab us a table."

Chloe had finally made her way to the counter, and I found one empty table tucked in the back corner, away from the line that went out the door.

The cafe was loud and alive with morning conversation, but this table was far enough away that we could probably hear each other without having to yell at each other.

I sipped my coffee as I waited for Chloe. I didn't know what the hell I was going to say to her, but we needed to talk.

She finally came over and sat down in the wooden chair across from me. "I clearly wasn't thinking when I volunteered to get coffee *and* breakfast for four people, knowing I have to carry it all back by myself."

"You're a good friend, Chloe. I'll help you carry that back to Wes's if you want."

"Thanks, but I'll manage."

I decided not to let the silence between us last any longer than it needed to. "Listen, Chloe, I—I really want to apologize to you for what happened in Vegas. I was way out of line."

Her shoulders lifted, then dropped as she sank back into her chair. "It's okay. We both were."

"Maybe, but I never should have put you in that position. And I damned sure didn't mean to ghost you. That was entirely unintentional."

"I get it now. We're both equally responsible for what happened that night. Now that I've had some time to process everything, I've pretty much pieced it all together. Between Wesley's accident, you somehow ending up being his friend, and now he's going to marry my best friend, I'm still having a hard time believing any of it's real. It's a lot to process."

I ran my hand through my hair. "Tell me about it. If it makes you feel any better, I did go back looking for you."

She shifted. "You did?"

130

I smiled at her. No way she believed I didn't. "Of course I did. I mean, after the night we had? Why wouldn't I? And we were less than sixty seconds away from officially sealing the deal when Warren called me to tell me about Wes's accident. I had no choice but to leave you…I just didn't realize until after I'd made it to the hospital that we hadn't swapped phone numbers." I let out a long breath. "By the time I made it back to the hotel, I had like less than three hours to pack all our stuff, look around for you, and make it to the airport."

She reached into one of her bags, picked a piece of danish, and ate it. "In your defense, you did tell me you'd be in touch. Never thought it would be like this."

"No shit. Again, I am so sorry."

"It's okay. Just so you know, I looked for you too. Well, I fell asleep in the lobby waiting for you to come back. You should have seen the look on the bellboy's face who had to wake me up and tell me to go to my room and go to bed. Then I overslept and by the time I woke up, it was later in the morning than I would have preferred before I finally made it back downstairs. I'm sure you were long gone by then."

"Yeah, I probably was."

"Well, I guess now that we got that all figured out, I'm sure you know then that we were never legally married."

I ran my hand through my hair. "I do know that. That was a crazy night though."

We talked some more about how each of us had found out on our own that our marriage wasn't legal. Crazy as it sounded, that was a hard pill to swallow. A part of me had kind of hoped it were real. Though I don't know what difference it would have made.

"I have a question for you," she said.

"Anything. Shoot."

"Do you prefer to go by Dan or Daniel?"

I let out a soft laugh. I knew she wasn't trying to be funny, but of all the questions she could have asked me, she wanted to know my name preference? "Everyone calls me Daniel. The only person that goes by Dan in my family is my dad. I don't know why that came out, but it did, and I just stuck with it."

"Interesting." She took a sip of her coffee.

"Let's just start over." I reached across the table and offered her my hand.

She tried to hide her smile as she gave her hand to me. "Okay. Sounds good."

"I'm Daniel Brown. Nice to meet you."

"Well, Daniel Brown, I'm Chloe Hill. It's nice to meet you."

"Chloe Hill, it's nice to meet you, too."

She looked me in the eyes, quietly waiting, her hand still in mine. It'd been what felt like a lifetime since I'd seen her or been this close to her, and I wanted to savor each second with her that I was given.

She pulled her hand away. "So how did your date go Friday night?"

*What the*—? *Friday*? "My date?"

"With Camilla?"

I laughed at the thought. "Camilla?" Our conversation had taken a drastic turn in the opposite direction I'd liked for it to go. "Oh man. We didn't—. I mean, we did go out together after we left Wes's, but it wasn't a date or anything like that."

"She sure looked like she was ready to go on a date." She stared down at her coffee cup, picking at the paper sleeve wrapped around it.

Unable to hide my amusement, I smirked, waiting for Chloe to look back up at me. "Do I sense a little jealousy?"

"No."

"No? Are you sure? Am I wrong?"

"Yes." She stood up to leave and started grabbing her stuff. "Look, I really need to go. Thanks for the talk, but we've been sitting here way too long and I'm pretty sure everyone's coffee is cold."

I stood up with her. If she was going to walk out on me mid-conversation, I was going with her. "At least let me help you carry all of that back."

"Thanks, but I can manage."

"Chloe, stop." I grabbed her wrist. "Listen. I'm not gonna lie. I fucked with her a long time ago. But not in years and damned sure not Friday night. Camilla is relentless in her chase. I'm used to it."

She relaxed in my grip and I let her go. "So y'all don't have anything going on?"

I shook my head. "No. Nothing. Camilla is just a drug rep that comes into the ER to sell us shit we don't need. That's her job. It just so happens that we sometimes see each other outside of work too because she and I hang out with the same people and sometimes at the same place to get away from the day-to-day corporate bullshit." A group of people pushed past us. "Besides, I already told you, I don't settle."

"Good to know. So what's it going to take then to get the 'forever and habitually single' Daniel Brown to drop anchor and settle down with one woman?"

She had a smirk on her face like she was taunting me, but I already knew Chloe wasn't ready for my answer, but I was dead serious. "You."

# SIXTEEN

## Daniel

You? *You*? Jesus. Of all the answers I could have given to Chloe to her question regarding what it would take for me to settle down, I tell her *you*.

The look of shock and confusion on her face told me all I'd needed to know. My answer was way out of line and had hit her out of left field, rendering her completely speechless…and not in a good way.

Without another word between us, I helped stack her two cup holders of coffee and two bags of food into her arms, before walking her out the door. She mumbled under her breath that she'd see me later tonight at Rowan's and disappeared in a sea of people.

In a matter of seconds, Chloe had me second-guessing what I'd thought would have been her appreciation for my straightforwardness. Maybe I'd completely misread her from the beginning. The only way I was ever going to find out would be to spend more one-on-one time with her but how the hell that was going to happen, I still didn't have a clue. But I was going to try.

I returned to my apartment almost an hour later. Shane was kicked back, watching TV. "Where the hell you been?" he asked as soon as I walked through the door.

"Sorry, man. I ran into a friend. Here." I handed him his blueberry muffin and went to the kitchen to heat up his coffee.

He flicked through the channels and ate his blueberry muffin. "It's all good. I figured something came up. What's the game plan for the rest of the day?"

I grabbed a bottle of water from the fridge and downed half of it. "Um, I gotta go to Wesley's later tonight. More wedding stuff. You wanna go?"

"Yeah, I'll go. Otherwise, I'll just be sitting here watching reruns of *The Walking Dead*."

"That doesn't sound like an awful night, actually. Are you back in the wedding? Do you know?" Originally, Wes had asked Shane to be in their wedding, too, but he'd backed out because he thought he wouldn't be able to take off work. Which ended up working out because that meant everyone had someone to walk with down the aisle. Otherwise, I would have been the single man out until Rowan could find someone to walk with me. Now with Shane back, she'd have to rework everything.

"Neither of them mentioned it, but I'm perfectly fine just having a front-row seat. I don't want to add to Rowan's stress."

"True. She kind of stays on edge these days. I'm sure her wheels started cranking as soon as you walked through the door."

"I don't wanna cause any problems. Ya know?"

I walked over and handed him his reheated coffee. "Guess we'll find out soon enough."

***

Shane and I made our way over to Wes's, and I was crazy nervous as hell about seeing Chloe for the first time since our breakfast debacle. She'd gotten away from me as fast as she could, and I felt like shit for scaring her away. That was the last thing I'd wanted.

As soon as we'd arrived at Wesley's, Rowan started talking wedding plans, confirming that she and Wes wanted Shane back in the wedding. Shane and everyone else, myself included, gave the okay. Not that we'd had a choice. I'd never tell a bride-to-be that she couldn't have her way with her own wedding.

"So," Rowan began—the whole crew was together, sitting around Wes's living room—"that puts Katie with Warren, Chloe walking with Shane, and Daniel...I've gotta find someone to walk with you, otherwise you're singled-out."

137

"I don't mind. I can walk alone or sit in the front row. Makes no difference to me. Hell, make me your flower girl. This is your wedding; you do whatever makes you happy. I'm just here for moral support."

She looked around searching for ideas from anyone who was willing to offer one up. No one said a word. So far Rowan hadn't been Bridezilla, but we weren't about to risk it now.

"Oh come on," she said. "Y'all know I don't have very many friends here, or any, for that matter. I only know like five people." She plopped down on Wes's lap with an exaggerated huff.

Wesley was the first one to speak up. "What about Camilla? I'm sure she wouldn't mind playing dress-up with you ladies."

Rowan bit her bottom lip. "You think she would? I mean, it's super last-minute. The wedding is in a week."

"Eh, might be worth a shot," Wesley encouraged her. "It wouldn't hurt to ask. I mean, that's if you want three couples. Otherwise, it'll just be the two, and we can find a different role for Daniel."

I thought asking Camilla to be in their wedding was a terrible idea because that would mean she and I would have to walk together. "I'm okay sitting this one out," I countered, hoping she wouldn't press the idea. "I don't want shit to get any more stressful for Rowan." Or me or Chloe. I was perfectly okay with Chloe walking with Shane, but my being in a wedding with Camilla was the last thing I'd wanted.

"No," Rowan said. "It's fine. Actually, that's not a bad idea. I'd prefer three couples. I know it sounds weird, but I really want an odd number of people on either side Wesley and me."

I felt Chloe's stare before I saw it. *Thanks, Wes.*

As if Chloe didn't already have her doubts about me and Camilla, even though I'd already told her otherwise, now she'd have to stand by and watch me walk down the aisle with her?

"Sounds like a plan, then. Daniel? Are you gonna be okay with that? If I can get Camilla on board?"

"I mean, yeah, whatever you need. I'm your man."

Rowan immediately called Camilla, extended an offer for her to be in their wedding, then asked if she was free to come over while she had everyone together. *Please be busy. Please be busy.* "Okay, its settled," she said as she hung up the phone. "Daniel, you're gonna walk down the aisle with Camilla."

Fucking wonderful. "Great." *Can't wait.*

My mood lightened as the night went on and things fell into place. Everything felt like it was getting back to normal…whatever that was. Chloe laughed more times than not, and she'd seemed to be enjoying herself. I didn't say any more dumb shit to make her not want to be in the same room as me, so that was nice.

Then Camilla showed up.

I mean, Rowan did invite her, but she never did mention one way or another whether or not Camilla was coming over to hang out tonight, and I didn't care enough to ask.

But what the fuck, Camilla? She waltzed in dressed unnecessarily for the runway, again. Even for her, it was a little over-the-top.

The air in the room felt dense, even though Chloe and I were probably the only two people who felt it.

As soon as Camilla sat down, Rowan picked up right where she'd left off, going over wedding plans, ironing out details for the rest of the week and day of the wedding. "I think this will really work out. Thanks, again, for volunteering on such short notice."

"It's my pleasure to help you out in any way I can. Let me know if you need anything else." She cut her eyes to me. "I'll make sure to leave everything wide-open for the next week."

*Oh, come on!* Could she make this shit anymore obvious?

"So, what are we going to wear?" Katie asked Rowan. "You said you narrowed it down to a few options. I liked all of the ones you've sent me."

"Well, the guys are all fitted and ready to go, except for Shane. Wesley can take him. Us girls will all go soon so we can pick out our dresses. I'm thinking sometime this weekend?"

Chloe piped in. "What about you? Isn't it kind of late in the game to be getting fitted for a wedding dress?"

"Oh, I'm already fitted for at least three. I just need y'all to help me pick one out. Y'all should be fine too. I have a few different styles set aside and already know the color. I'll leave it up to each of y'all to pick your own style of dress. And the shop has a guy who's on standby for a rush job, if anyone needs their dress tailored."

Camilla gave Chloe a low-key side-eye.

Shit like this was exactly why I preferred to stay single. Life was far less complicated. It was bad enough I had one woman I knew without a doubt wanted me and a second woman I hoped felt the same. The one I had zero interest in, I had to see on a regular basis. The other one I was crazy about but wasn't entirely convinced I'd ever see her again once she left town. Now both of them were together in the same room as me, which had already occurred two times too many.

As the women drank wine and carried on, Wesley, Warren, and Shane went out on to the balcony, probably to enjoy the silence and light up a cigar. I headed to the butler pantry and raided Wesley's liquor cabinet. "Bingo."

"Find what you're looking for?"

I jumped at the sound of the voice but didn't need to look to know who it was. "Indeed, I did. You want some?" I held up a bottle of Patrón.

"Not my drink of choice. I'll pass." Camilla walked up beside me, closing in on the already tight space, wedging herself between me and the door. "What's with that woman out there?" she said, nodding the direction of the living room toward the laughter. "You two seem…cozy tonight."

*Not cozy enough.* "If you're talking about Chloe, that's none of your business." The already small space felt like it was closing in as Camilla blocked the exit.

See, the thing about Camilla was she was used to getting her way. She was cutthroat by nature, and with her being in sales in a man's world, she had to work extra hard to get what she wanted. Even if that meant her working the men themselves—myself included. Other than that one-time years ago, I'd never caved into any of her advances. She wasn't used to hearing the word "no." But I had to give her an A for effort.

"You know we were good together once."

"Once. It was one time and one time only. That was the rule. Nothing has changed."

"Oh, I see a lot has changed."

142

"Maybe. We'll see. Now, if you'll excuse me? Please."

Surprisingly, she stepped to the side without further resistance, leaving me just enough room to squeeze between her and the door frame.

"There you are!" A glassy-eyed Chloe walked up to me just as I exited the kitchen with Camilla hot on my heels. "Oh, sorry, I didn't know you were busy."

I never lost eye contact with Chloe as Camilla passed by, rejoining the others. "I wasn't. Not in the least bit. But I did find this." I held up the Patrón.

She smirked at the sight of the bottle.

"It's not top-shelf, but it'll get the job done."

She bit her bottom lip, and I almost came undone. It was the most unmistakably flirty she had been with me since we'd reconnected.

I rubbed the pad of my thumb across her lip. "Fuck I wish I could do that," I whispered under my breath just loud enough for her to hear me.

She snatched the bottle from my grip, popped off the cork top, took a shot straight from the bottle, and handed it back to me. "One more of those and I might let you."

"Glad to see you're drinking again." I looked around the room. Everyone seemed to be distracted with either food, conversation, or alcohol. So I grabbed Chloe's hand and pulled her down the hallway into a

143

place I knew I could get her alone for even just a few minutes.

She stumbled to catch her footing behind me. "Where are we—?"

"Shh."

Glancing back over my shoulder, making sure the coast was still clear, I gave her a nudge ahead of me and closed the door, locking us in the dark room. Not that we really needed to hide from anyone. We were two grown, consenting adults. But it was more out respect for Rowan and the fact that Chloe was her best friend. I didn't need Rowan thinking I was only after her for only one thing.

I set the bottle down on the nightstand, shoved the cork back in place, and flicked on the bedside light. "Come here."

She strolled over to me, and I finally took her into my arms. The smell of liquor mixed with her sweet perfume hung in the air between us. I looked down at her—well, at the top of her head. "What are you, like four foot ten?"

She poked her finger into my rib cage, causing me to jump, then she pinched my nipple. "Ouch. What was that for?"

"Payback. And it's eleven and a half," she said with a huff, looking up at me with her chest all puffed out—like she'd really needed to. Those things entered the room before she did.

Chloe was a mouthy little shit, and odd as it was, it was a huge fucking turn-on. She was a whole lot of fire and spice and everything I'd ever wanted in a woman and never knew I'd needed. The last thing I'd wanted was to try to tame her. But I was ready for whatever burn she was going to give me.

"You know you sure talk a lot of shit for someone who can't reach the middle shelf of an upper cabinet."

"Is that why you locked me in here with you? So you could give me crap about my height?"

"Not in the least bit. I needed a few minutes alone with you."

"Hmm. Well, you talk a lot of game for someone with a seemingly *decent dick* he doesn't want to use," she said to me in a sarcastic tone, mocking my words.

I squeezed her tight, pressed my seemingly *decent dick* into her front and grazed my mouth against her ear. "Whoever said I didn't want to use it?"

She wrapped her arms around my waist. "You did. In Vegas."

"Good point. And while I did deny you the pleasure back then, that didn't mean I didn't *want* to bend you over and bury my dick deep inside of you. Because *that* was exactly what I had planned on doing until Warren called me. Otherwise, I would have. I already told you that."

She let out a soft moan as she melted in my arms. "So what's stopping you now?"

"The fact that we're standing in Wes and Rowan's guest bedroom with a room full of people less than twenty feet away. And neither of us can seem to catch a fucking break away from this wedding shit to be alone together long enough to do anything."

"True."

"But I'll make it up to you."

She dropped her forehead into my chest. "Promise?"

I rubbed my hand up and down her back. "Eventually, yes."

"If you say so."

"Chloe?"

"Hmm?" She looked up at me and I cupped her face in my hands. Then I leaned down and firmly, but gently, pressed my lips to hers without wasting another second with her. When she didn't pull away or kick me in the balls, I slid my tongue across her lips, nudging my way inside. Her opened up for me, and as soon as she let me in, I devoured her mouth with my own.

After what felt like forever, I reluctantly forced myself to break our kiss, both of us completely winded. "I do say so. And don't ever refer to my dick as *decent*

Lyndsay Marie

again. I'll have no choice but to show you just how
sufficient it is."

# SEVENTEEN

*Daniel*

The longest three days of my life were waiting to find out if I'd been accepted into med school, finding out where I'd been matched, and the length of time it'd been since I'd last seen or talked to Chloe. I could not believe how much of a pussy I'd become when it came to her, how I'd somehow let myself fall victim to those annoying little things called *feelings*. Even more surprising was how little I cared about what was even happening to me.

"Earth to Daniel."

"Yeah, what? I'm as present as ever."

"Dude, you're more distant than these women who were supposed to be here over ten minutes ago."

"Oh, yeah, where are they?" I asked like I didn't care that they were late, but truth be told, the longer they took, the more anxious I became.

Lyndsay Marie

"I just texted Rowan a few minutes ago. She said they were on their way. She also said that the first time I messaged her."

Wesley had unknowingly reminded me I still didn't have Chloe's phone number. That would be remedied today. She was not leaving my sight until we swapped contact info. At this point, I was ready to send her a carrier pigeon.

No sooner than I thought about all of the dirty little messages I could be sending her, the woman who was quickly turning into my most favorite person walked through the door. Leave it to her to show up dressed like some sexy librarian or secretary. Now all I'd be able to think about was bending her over this dining room table.

I adjusted my dick under the table as Chloe walked in behind Rowan and Katie, soon followed by none other than the vixen herself, Camilla. Of course she'd entered last and a few feet behind the others. Camilla wanted all eyes on her.

But not mine. They were locked in on one woman and one woman only.

My mouthy little firecracker.

Rowan greeted Wesley then made all of us guys get up so she could rearrange where she wanted everyone to sit. I had the un-fucking-believable misfortune of sitting smack-dab between what should

149

have been every man's wet dream but given my circumstances had the potential of turning into a nightmare. Camilla crowded me on one side, Chloe the other.

We sat uncomfortably—well at least I did—as we ate lunch and knocked back a few much-needed drinks. A couple of times I had to scoot my chair away from Camilla because, whether or not it was intentional, she was inching hers closer to mine. Although, I didn't mind moving because it meant my getting closer to Chloe. But at one point, Camilla had set her hand on my thigh under the table, and I almost came unglued. She hadn't been this brazen in a long time, and her antics were starting to piss me off.

As lunch wound down, we all stood and stretched. A few people made their way outside for fresh air, Camilla being one of them and *thank fuck*.

Warren checked his watch. "What's the plan tonight, Daniel?"

*Shit. Really, Warren*? He wanted to talk about tonight now? It was awkward enough discussing my Friday night plans around Chloe once; I didn't want to do it again. "Haven't thought that far ahead." *Asshole*.

Chloe excused herself to the bathroom, my assumption was to avoid overhearing our conversation.

"Well, you bailed out on me early last weekend. You going for round two?"

Lyndsay Marie

"I'll have to see what the rest of the afternoon has in store."

"You created this monster," Wesley said to me. "Don't start dicking around and leaving him off his leash unattended now."

"For fuck's sake. Warren is a grown man. He doesn't need me to get laid."

"I didn't say I needed you to get laid, but it's nice to have a wingman, Doc," he said with a wink.

"Smart-ass. We'll talk about tonight later. I gotta piss." I loosened the collar of my shirt as I casually strolled across the restaurant to the far corner, heading to the bathroom. As soon as I rounded the corner down the hall, I ran straight into Chloe as she stepped out of the women's bathroom, which was exactly what I'd hoped for.

I caught her under her arm as I moved past her, spun her around and dragged her into a dim, empty banquet hall. "I'm not done with you yet."

"Oh? Is that so? How do you have time for me if you're out with Warren getting laid?"

"I already told you where I was last weekend."

"Yeah, with Camilla and Warren—oh, did y'all have some kind of three-way thing going on?"

I yanked her across the room behind a wall of folded-up tables, gripping the top of one of them, caging her between my arms. "I'm going to pretend like you

151

didn't just ask me that," I said, looking her dead in the eyes, "but I gotta ask you, Chloe, are you as into me now as you were in Vegas? Or was that just a miserably failed one-night stand that ended with a fake marriage, and now you're just trying to push me away? Or are you scared?" She swallowed hard. *That's what I thought.* "Because my feelings for you, whatever the hell they are anymore, have not changed. And every time I see you only confirms to me that I'm not as crazy as I'd initially thought I was, or maybe I am. But if you really don't want me, just say the word. I'll stop pursuing you and move on, like I probably should've done over a year ago." And not because I wanted to.

Chloe responded by wrapping her fingers around my belt and pulling me even closer into her. "I'm not pushing *you* away."

"I don't want you to." Bracing myself with one hand, I reached behind her, cupped her ass and squeezed it hard. "Am I still what you want, Chloe?"

She closed her eyes, dropping her head back against the table. Her lips parted as her breathing became more rapid. She didn't have to say a word—the way she responded without her voice told me everything I needed to know.

I dipped my head down, planting a soft kiss on the side of her neck. She turned her head to the side, exposing more skin for me to access. I kissed her again, and again, as I worked my way up to the corner of her jawline, just below her ear.

"You know what I want," she said in a ragged whisper.

I smiled against her delicate skin.

With one hand still holding tight on to her ass, I dropped my other hand to one of her large, half-exposed mounds of cleavage and squeezed her tit through the sheer material of her flimsy white blouse and lacy bra. "I have half a mind to rip this shirt right off of you."

She let out a whimper. "We—we should go before we get caught." The tug I felt on my belt, drawing me even closer into her, told me she wanted otherwise. Then she smiled against my lips.

Without wasting any more time, I took her mouth with mine.

This time it wasn't soft and nice and sweet. There was no holding back or giving her time to wonder what I wanted. My message was loud and clear. This was a kiss of need and passion—the kind where teeth clink together and your rhythm is off, but you don't give a shit. You keep on going.

She tried reaching her hand down the front of my pants, but my belt was on too tight, so she opted for rubbing my rock-hard dick through my dress pants instead.

Our mouths never lost contact as our hands roamed and grabbed and rubbed on whatever we could reach. I slid my hand from her ass up under the hem of her skirt to the inside of her thigh. She moaned and whispered unintelligible words into my mouth as we kissed.

I pulled away, trying to catch my breath, dropping my forehead onto hers. "May I?" I needed to hear her give me permission to go any further with her, even though I was pretty damned convinced we both wanted the same thing.

She shook her head. "Yes. Safe. IUD."

That was all I needed to hear. "Fuck, Chloe." I rubbed her on her pussy through the outside of the lacy material, my fingers not yet touching her skin. "You are so fucking hot and so goddamned wet."

She rocked her hips into my hand. "Daniel. I need to come. If you don't do it, I will."

"Don't tell me that," I growled into her ear. My cock tensed in need of release, but the throbbing pain I felt was worth every second I had with her.

"I know you don't think as many times as you've left me horny that I've just been carrying on this whole time needing an orgasm?"

I let out a low growl, then pushed her panties to the side and slid my fingers beneath the fabric between her legs. I'd barely touched the tip of my finger over her clit when she let out a moan that I was sure could be heard clear on the other side of the other room.

Instinctively, I covered her mouth with my free hand. "Shh. Fuck. I want to hear that pretty little mouth of yours screaming, but not here. Not now."

She nodded, a promise to keep quiet.

I uncovered her mouth and wrapped my hand around her waist, my fingers still barely breaching her entrance.

I teased her, running the length of my fingers back and forth, from front to back, pressing my palm against her clit.

As I taunted and teased her, she started jacking me off through the outside of my pants. Then, I felt her other hand on mine between her legs. "You're taking too fucking long," she said as she pushed my fingers deep inside of her.

That was all it took. I worked hard and fast on her. She panted as she squeezed and rubbed my dick even harder. Her dripping wet pussy tensed around my fingers. I threw my mouth over hers to catch her moans and cries.

Just as I was sure she was coming, I heard someone calling out. "Yo, D. Where are you? You coming? We gotta go."

*Fuuuuck. Yeah, I would be if you hadn't interrupted me.*

We broke our kiss, both jerking our heads toward voice on the far side of the room. Thank God if anyone had walked in they never would have seen us hidden behind the folded-up tables, but we still had to somehow get the hell out of there unseen.

"I'm so sorry." I slowly pulled my fingers out of her, careful not to touch her dark-colored skirt. "I owe you big-time."

"So what's new? And who was that?" she asked, straightening herself out while watching me as I licked my fingers clean of her.

"Warren. We've both been MIA for a minute."

"Yeah, no shit." She gave the front of her shirt and skirt a once-over. "How do I look?"

I brushed her hair back in place with my clean hand. "You're beautiful, Chloe."

Even in the dark room, lit only by a little bit of summer sunlight that poured from behind the curtains, I could still see her bright smile. "Thank you. But can we go now? I need to get back to Rowan's and figure out how I'm going to finish what you started."

I leaned down and gave her one more soft, lingering kiss. "Ladies first."

We made our way back into the main dining area. "There you...two...are," Rowan called out, her voice trailing off, as Chloe and I reappeared.

Lyndsay Marie

"I'll, uh, meet you in the car, Rowe." Chloe scampered away, heading for the front door, adjusting her skirt in the process.

Rowan smacked my arm.

"What the—?"

"Stop ogling her like she's a strip of bacon and you haven't eaten in a week."

"Wha—I can't. Never mind." It wasn't worth the argument to find the right words to defend myself against gawking at Rowan's best friend. She'd busted me free and clear.

Rowan shoved my arm, spinning me around, and shielded herself from anyone seeing the tongue-lashing I had no doubt I was about to receive. "Daniel Brown," she scolded me in a hushed tone. "I'm serious. I know how you are, and I am on to you. Do not fuck with my best friend. Because if you hurt her, I will kill you. Dead."

"Rowan. You need to chill. I am not *fucking* with your best friend. I happen to like Chloe. And as it turns out, I'm starting to think she kind of feels the same about me."

"Those are pretty bold words for someone who's a self-proclaimed man-whore."

"Well, I mean, yeah, I am, but people change. And I know a good woman when I see one."

She blew out a deep breath and relaxed a little. "I just worry about her. I know she's a big girl, and God knows she can damned sure hold her own, but she's been through a lot, and the last thing I want to see is her getting hurt again. Especially by you."

I pulled Rowan into a hug. "I assure you, Rowan, the last thing I want to do is hurt Chloe. You have my word."

"Good. Now whatever this shit is between you and Camilla, end it. I already know there's a history there, and I'm sorry y'all have to walk together in the wedding, but let that be the last of it if you're going to continue whatever it is you and Chloe are up to. Please."

"I'll take care of it." Because sooner or later, I fully intended on taking care of her friend, too, and in more ways than one.

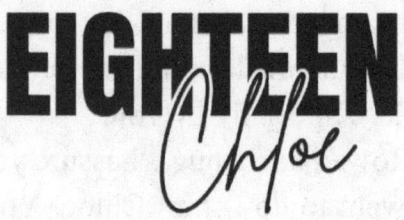

# EIGHTEEN
## Chloe

Friggin' Daniel. What the hell? He sure had a knack for turning me on and leaving me furiously horny and frustrated. So far we were zero out of what felt like way too attempts at getting any further than second base. As sexy as that was, I was about to go out of my damned mind. Not only because we'd had a very few opportunities to start with, but our time together was dwindling away fast. We had one week and one day to make something, *anything*, happen.

I wanted to scream and rip my hair out.

"All right, ladies. Who wants a drink? Kat? Chlo? Water? Wine? Anyone?" Rowan asked us while bustling around her kitchen, seemingly looking for nothing in particular.

Kat raised her hand. "I'll take a glass of wine. But not too much. I know how you like to pour."

"What? I'm a generous person." She pulled two long-stemmed wine glasses out of a cabinet. "Anything in particular? Red? White? Pink?"

"Surprise me."

"Chloe?" Rowan asked me. "What about you? You want a glass?"

A glass of wine did sound nice. Something to help me unwind, take the edge of the day off…my mind off Daniel. "Eh, Maybe a small touch of something later."

"Suit yourself." Rowan poured Kat some wine and handed it to her, then put the empty glass away.

"Where's yours, Rowan? You not drinking one? Y'all wanna talk about me not drinking. This one here hasn't had a drop of alcohol since we've been here."

"Can't. Still on meds for this crazy UTI. Y'all know me…Miss Play it Safe."

I grabbed Kat's glass out of her hand just as she was about to take a sip.

"Hey, hooker," she said, swatting at my hand. "Get your own."

I took a fast sip before she caused me to spill it and handed it back to her. "I'm not a hooker, hooker. And I don't want my own glass. That's what I have yours for."

"Well, Chloe knows how to make her own drink, if she changes her mind."

"Whatever. So, what's on the agenda tonight?" I asked. "Anything in particular you wanna discuss or go over?"

"Not really. Thought we'd take a night off from the wedding. I know y'all are probably tired of talking about it. Plus, I'm feeling kinda blah, and we have a ton of stuff to do over the next week."

"Where's Camilla tonight?" Kat asked. "You didn't invite her to hang out with us?"

"I didn't really have anything planned other than just hanging out here. She told me unless I needed her, she had something else going on and she'd just catch up with us tomorrow."

I had no problems with taking a night off from Camilla. My problem was the only time I seemed to have seen her was when Daniel was around, which likely meant if I didn't want to see her, I'd probably have to go without seeing him too.

*Well, shit.* Now I wondered if they were out together somewhere. I hated the thought, and I still didn't have his damn phone number, or I'd text him and see. Having my own drink was sounding better and better.

"I'll tell you what I do want to do at some point…maybe," I said, probably sounding just as deflated as I felt.

"What's that?" Rowan asked.

"I'd like to go out." At this point, I *needed* to get out. "I really want to see this city at night. Not that your place isn't amazing." Because their penthouse was just as spectacular as the view from every window. "But I've been itching to go and do a little exploring." It was one thing to get a glimpse of life below, but it was an entirely different experience to see it from the ground up.

"Well, don't let me stop you. If you're gonna go do anything, tonight's probably your best bet. We have a busy week ahead. Just don't forget, dress shopping in the morning."

"We can't leave you," Kat said as she jabbed her elbow into my side. "Can we?"

"Of course not, Rowan." I smacked Kat back on her thigh. "We'll stay in and help you work out any last-minute kinks." Though, I could easily think of a few kinks I had of my own that needed to be worked out, and they had nothing to do with weddings or wine or dresses or anything either of them could do for me.

"Chloe, I know you way too well. You've been in a new city for a week, cooped up. I know you're dying to go do *something* nightlife."

She wasn't wrong. But I wasn't here for me. "It's okay, really. I can come back to vacation any time I want. This trip is all about you."

"Oh puh-lease. If it were me, I'd leave you. Just don't go far. Neither of y'all know your way around."

"Y'all? Don't bring me into this mess. I'm not leaving you or going anywhere."

Rowan rolled her eyes. "Right, Kat. But neither of us are going to let this one"—she nodded toward me—"go out alone in freaking downtown Chicago."

Wesley strolled up out of nowhere. "Who's going out alone in downtown Chicago?"

"No one," I said. "Nobody is going nowhere. Y'all aren't blaming this one on me. Just because I said I'd *like* to go out, doesn't mean I *am*."

"Kat. Get your girl. Take her out but don't wander off too far. There's a few classy places close by y'all might like."

Wesley wrapped his arms around Rowan, hugging her from behind. It was the sweetest thing, watching the two of them together. Also kinda made me sick…but in a good way. "You sure that's a good idea? Letting these two out into the wild unsupervised?"

"I assure you, between the two of them, they can handle it. Trust me. There's plenty of trouble for them to get into in a two-block radius of here." She looked back and forth between Kat and me. "Seriously, you won't even need to take an Uber back. We'll plan for our last girls' night closer to the wedding…like next Friday?"

Rowan didn't need to convince me any more than I'd already convinced myself that I really wanted a night away. I was sold.

I looked at Kat who looked like she was just as anxious and giddy as me to get out for a little while and not discuss anything wedding. "Okay…okay!" Kat said, polishing off her wine. "We'll go. But only for a little while, and promise we'll stay close."

I rounded the kitchen island, shoved Wesley out of my way, and kissed Rowan on the cheek. "What are you going to do? You wanna go?"

"Oooh, no. I'm not up for going anywhere."

"She's going to sit here with me and Shane and suffer through stories from when we were teens, then pass out on the couch before ten," Wesley said.

"Come on, let's go before Mother Hen changes her mind." I ran over, grabbed Kat, and dragged her toward the door. "Don't wait up," I yelled to Rowan.

"Trust me. I wasn't planning on it. Y'all have fun and be safe. And don't stay out too late," she called out as the door closed behind us.

As soon as the elevator hit the ground floor and the doors slid open, Kat and I were on our phones scouting out nearby restaurants and bars.

"Here's one. It's right over there," Kat said, pointing almost directly across the street.

"Nah. Too close." I pulled up another bar that was a little further away. "How about this one? Looks like they have karaoke and it's right around the corner."

She skimmed through the pics on my screen. "Looks like dive-bar and I am not in the mood for karaoke."

"Well, let's start walking and see what we come up with that isn't within our two-block radius limit."

"How about three?" She handed me her phone.

"Huh. Seems kinda swanky." The place she showed me was the complete opposite of a dive-bar with its high-end crystal light fixtures, dim mood lighting, and everything covered in polished brass, wood, and leather.

She grabbed her phone from my grip. "Swanky sounds perfect. Let's go."

We walked more than two city-blocks away from our promised one and then three more. "I hope you know where the hell we're going."

"Just following Google."

It wasn't much longer and we were finally walking into one of the fanciest places that had no business calling themselves a bar, that I'd ever stepped foot inside.

Before we made our way through a second set of double doors, a bouncer stopped us to check our IDs and collect our entry fee.

"I had no idea Chicago was this damn expensive. If they charge that much to get in, I can't imagine what they expect me to pay for drinks."

"Judging by the quality of men that just left, I'm willing to bet it's worth it. With any luck we'll find someone else to pay for them, anyway."

I sure as hell hoped so.

We stood just inside the main entrance and scanned the room. Most of the tables were already occupied, and so were all the over-stuffed leather sofas in a sectioned-off seating area in the middle of the room.

*What the hell kind of place did Katie bring me to?*

"This place is fancy as fuck," I said out loud, more to myself than anything. From what I could tell, the majority, if not all of the patrons, were way overdressed and a far cry from the folks I was used to seeing back home, even on a good day. Every man from what I could see was sporting some form of *GQ*-looking businesslike attire; the women were decked out to the nines in dresses that were extra short, tops that were exceptionally tight, and shoes with heels taller than even my own. I was still wearing the outfit I'd had on at brunch. Not that I looked like a dumpster fire in comparison, but what I had one was not up to par for keeping up with these people.

"I think our safest best for now is the bar."

I followed her lead as we grabbed two empty, full-sized leather chairs—not barstools—at the bar. Within seconds, a bartender approached us out of nowhere, and took our drink orders.

"That was fast," Kat said. No sooner than she'd said the words, the bartender returned in record time with our drinks. "We don't get that kinda service back home."

"That's because we don't have these kinda places back home, either." Not that I knew of, anyway. Quite frankly I was surprised they'd even let us in the door.

We sipped and people-watched. If it weren't for my most recent and unexpected distraction—AKA Daniel—I'd have been all over the opportunities that walked around us.

Instead, my mind wandered back to him. It always did. I tried hard to fight that shit off too but no matter what I thought about, everything went back to him. I mean, here we were, another Friday night, and I couldn't help but let curiosity get the best of me and wonder where he was or what or *who* he was doing. I had my doubts that he'd actually be sitting at home. Deep down, I'd hoped to somehow run into him tonight, but what were the odds? We were in downtown Chicago—he could literally be a million different places.

"Have you heard anything from Rowan yet?"

"No, but I haven't checked, either." I dug through my purse for my phone and pulled out a random napkin stuck at the bottom. "What the?"

"What is it? Something wrong?"

"No. Nothing. Couldn't find my phone." I held it up to show her. "Found it." And a white napkin with Daniel's name and what I assumed was his phone number written on it. *When the hell did he slip that in there?*

"Shit. That is strong," Kat said, in between sips of her drink. "Can I just say, I, for one, am glad to see you've decided to start drinking again. I've missed my drinking partner."

I shrugged. "Guess I needed to take a break. Really, it was no big deal. I think better when my head is clear. Plus, I don't find myself sending late-night texts to exes who have no business still having their number in my phone."

She raised her glass in a toast. "True that. And speaking of exes, you aren't talking to Tanner again, are you? Please tell me you're not."

"Not at all. I haven't heard from him in months, believe it or not." Tanner and I had started dating more seriously after I got home from Vegas. Things between us weren't *terrible*. He was genuinely a nice guy, but that was about as far as things between us went. Our first problem was the poor guy couldn't give a woman an orgasm if you boxed it up and tied it up with a bow. Our second problem? He'd apparently been a virgin, and he'd let me defile him. After several unsuccessful romps in the sack, he'd finally admitted his little secret. Shit was all downhill from there. I'd stuck that one out for as long as I could, but I'd run out of excuses to not sleep with him anymore, and nice only goes so far.

"Good. Maybe he finally moved on. What a clusterfuck that one was."

"Hey! You're one to talk about cluster-fucks and moving on. What's Justin up to these days?"

"For your information," she said with all the confidence she had within her as she sat up tall and poised, "I wouldn't know."

"Oh really? How long has it been this time? One week? Two months?"

Her posture deflated. "Twelve days."

"Ha! I knew it. What was it this time?"

"I wanted to come on this trip and not be bombarded with phone calls and text messages and emails, all checking in, asking me what I was doing, who I was with, or when I was going not be out and about. In case you didn't know, it's a hell of a lot of work to keep up with all that. Not to mention mentally exhausting for me to listen to it all."

169

"Considering y'all have been doing this back-and-forth shit for well over, what, four years? I'm glad you chose now to take a break. Are you happy with your decision?"

She smiled a soft, genuine smile. "I am. It feels good this time. Like, it was the right thing to do, ya know?"

Boy, did I ever. "Yeah, I do. But for how long?"

She stared down at her glass. "I don't know. Hopefully ever."

We both knew better.

I finished off my second strong cocktail and ordered a third. As I drank this one down a little faster than the one before it, a familiar flush of warmth coursed through my veins, and it was just enough to give me a jolt of courage I needed to finally tap out a text to Daniel.

No sooner than I'd hit Send, two random guys popped up from seemingly out of nowhere, flanking Kat and me on either side, squishing us together.

"Ladies," one of them said. "Good evening. Or good night. Depending."

The other dude leaned on the bar, taking up Kat's personal space. "Sup."

"Hi," she said back with a look of disgust on her face. He was close enough she had probably smelled his breath.

"Hey" was all I could muster under my breath.

Okay, so out of every possible swinging dick this place had to offer, we get approached by these two douchebags, with their slicked-back hair and tufts of chest hair poking through the collar of their shirts? I'd definitely lost my touch if this were how things were going to be going for me, that or Chicago had a hell of a lot less to offer than I'd thought.

The guy beside me nodded at my half-empty martini glass. He had to be at least twice my age. "What're you drinking there, sweetheart? Can I get you another one?"

I looked down at my drink, shielding the top with my hand. "Cosmo," I replied in the flattest tone possibly. Even in my most desperate hour, I'd have never gone for this dude or his drinks. He reeked of used-car salesman and cheap cologne. I was willing to bet the bouncer doubled his entry fee.

"You two ladies here alone? 'Cause, uh, I don't see no one else around." Kat shifted uncomfortably in her seat, scooting closer to me as the guy talked, probably spraying spittle into her drink.

"For now," Kat said. "We're meeting someone."

The guy beside me reached up, grabbing a lock of my hair, and twirling it between his fingers. "You sure? You two been sitting here a while by yourselves.

171

If your friend doesn't show up, you two are welcome to leave with us."

My glass trembled under my hand. Kat and I were closed in and had nowhere to go. Worst case, I'd scream for the bartender, but I didn't have to. A third deep—but familiar voice—sounded behind me.

"Ladies. Sorry I'm late."

Lyndsay Marie

# NINETEEN

*Daniel*

To say this was the longest it had ever taken me to get laid by one single female would be the understatement of my life, possibly this century. Then again, I never usually pursued a woman for this long, or made this many attempts. But damn, I wanted Chloe, and ever since our little encounter at rehearsal lunch, I would stop at damn near nothing to have her.

"So, what made you change your mind about coming out tonight? I half expected you to bail on me again."

Warren and I sat in our usual spot in the middle of what had once, not so very long ago, been my favorite go-to place for everything I needed. Unfortunately, or maybe it was a blessing in disguise, but this shit was all very quickly turning into a thing of the past. "I wouldn't say I changed my mind."

"Ah, so you weren't going to ghost on me again tonight? I really thought you were."

173

"Oh, no, I still plan on it. I'm just here for a drink or two, then I'm bouncing out."

"Where do you plan on going from here? Home?" He leaned forward, propping his elbows on his knees. "Because I distinctly remember a time not very long ago when you were the one who had to convince *me* to get out of my apartment; now here I am trying to get you to stay up past ten? What gives?"

I knew damned well what my problem was, and she'd spent the past week just out of arm's reach, which drove me abso-fucking-lutely insane. "Just things," I said in a casual tone, trying to avoid eye contact with him, along with any more questioning.

"Christ. Even I couldn't have come up with a more lame excuse than that." He sat back and casually kicked his feet up on the wooden coffee table between us. "Well, what or whoever it is that's got you in this fog, I can't say I'm fully against it."

"What? Why?"

"This," he said, waving his hand dismissively around the room, "is honestly getting old, or hell, maybe I'm the one getting old."

"Wait a minute"—I put my hand up—"aren't you the one who not thirty seconds ago was giving me shit for bailing on you last week? Now you're telling me you want to call it an early night?"

"I said it was getting old, not that I wanted it to end, necessarily. But coming here on a regular basis has made it difficult for me to get any real work done. Plus I really just enjoy giving you shit."

His admission to essentially not being able to keep up with me made me laugh. He'd barely started coming out with me on a *regular basis* a few months ago. Now he was ready to throw in the towel? "Fucker. I told you. And Wes told you. Hell, I'm pretty sure Rowan warned you. It ain't easy being me, that's for damned sure. But I'm impressed you've held out this long. Most wingmen would have quit by now."

Our waitress approached us with our fresh drinks before Warren had a chance to come back with some smart-ass response.

I relaxed back into the leather sofa, mirroring Warren, refill in hand, and absorbed my surroundings of a place that had become like a second home for me. Odd as it was, it did bring a certain comfort to me.

Then, as if the gates of heaven had opened themselves up and sent me my own personal angel, I spotted Chloe from across the room—well, I saw Katie, first, towering over Chloe by almost a foot. But there was no mistaking Chloe. As soon as I'd laid my eyes on her, she was all I could see anymore.

What in the hell were they doing here?

I watched them as they looked around the room before deciding to settle in at the bar. It didn't seem like they were looking for anyone in particular because I knew damned well that them being here was sheer coincidence. And a very happy one, at that.

As I kept an eagle eye on Chloe, another familiar face broke into my line of sight, blocking my view, heading straight toward me.

*You've got to be shitting me.*

She was the last person I wanted to see, and the longer shit went on with her, the more I'd come to realize just how bad my decision to hook up with her to begin with had been. The hard-to-get game was fun in the beginning. I mean, what man wouldn't want some curvaceous, Puerto Rican princess chasing after his dick? My problem was now, she would not take no for an answer, and her pursuit had become relentless. Now this shit was just getting on my nerves. And after my chat with Rowan, I knew this had to end tonight.

Warren laughed, failing miserably at trying to hide behind his glass of scotch, as Camilla approached us.

"Gentlemen. It's good to see you two out."

"Considering we're here almost every week," I said, "that shouldn't surprise you." Camilla had known exactly where, when, and how to find me. Hell, she'd

176

practically made a habit of making her presence known at this point.

She had a cocky grin on her face as she turned to look directly at me. "And where is your girlfriend, Daniel?"

"I wouldn't know. I don't have one."

"Interesting. She must not be putting out for you, *yet*."

Her emphasis on the word *yet* really irritated at me; hell, *she* irritated me. "I'm curious, Camilla, at what point are you going to stand down from this and move on? Because I—."

She cut me off. "You mean to bigger and better?" Then she rolled her eyes and took a sip of her drink.

Warren sat quietly with his own drink in hand, seemingly minding his own business, but his raised eyebrow let me know damned good and well he'd been listening to every word of this conversation.

"Good luck with that."

"Don't flatter yourself. And who said I was even here for you?"

"Touché." It was time to shut this shit down. "Hey, you know, Camilla, I read somewhere that orgasms were good for your health."

She cocked her head to the side. "Is that so?"

"Yeah, so if I ever tell you to go fuck yourself, it's only because I care about your well-being."

Warren sat up, practically spitting out his drink. He started to stand and looked like he was going to make a beeline for the door. *No way, buddy. You're not going anywhere.* I stood up before he did and took a dramatic bow.

Warren stopped mid-stance, stunned. "Where are you going?"

I smiled at him. "If you need me, I'll be at the bar." I walked away, leaving him to his own defense with Camilla.

I didn't give a fuck at this point if anyone knew where I was going or who I was going after. I knew what I wanted, and I was going to get it.

I pushed past Camilla, and as I approached the bar, the two guys I'd noticed earlier had made their way to Chloe and Katie.

"No fucking way. Not tonight." I walked up behind Chloe and placed both my hands on her shoulders. She jumped in her seat. "It's just me," I whispered in her ear. "Ladies, sorry I'm late."

The two guys looked me up and down, grumbled some shit under their breath, grabbed their drinks, and walked off without another word. Thank fuck because I knew damned well there was no way I could take them both on by myself.

I leaned against the bar beside Chloe. She looked terrified and relieved at the same time. "What are you two doing here? Did Wesley put you up to this?"

They looked at each other, then back at me. "Wesley? No. Why?"

"Just a hunch."

Chloe looked around me. "Are you here alone?"

"No. Warren is here." I nodded toward the middle of the room. "He's just on the other side of that half wall. I'm sure he'd enjoy some company."

"Oh! Okay, well, let me tab out. We'll go over there."

Chloe went to pull out her wallet. I grabbed her wrist to stop her. "I didn't mean all of us." I looked up at her friend then back at her. "I was talking about Katie."

Katie jerked her head up. "What? Me?"

"Oooh," Chloe said. "Yeah, Kat, go see what Warren is doing. We'll be right here."

"I got your tab. I'm sure he'll be happy to see you," I told Katie, reassuring her, giving her a little nudge to go see him for a while so I could have Chloe alone.

After a few seconds of internal debate and a wordless exchange with Chloe, Katie grabbed her things without any objection and made her way to Warren. Hopefully by the time she got to him, Camilla would be gone. Then again, maybe that's what his ass needed, to be put into an awkward situation. Let him sort it out on his own. The thought was amusing.

Chloe watched as her friend disappeared to the other side of the partitioning wall that Warren was sitting behind. "Well, that explains why I didn't see y'all when we walked in…not that I was looking for you or anything."

I grabbed the empty leather chair behind me, scooted it as close to Chloe as I could, and sat down. "Doesn't matter, I saw you."

"And you've just been watching me this whole time?"

"Maybe. So how did you find this place? It's a little out of the way from where you guys are staying."

"Google. We needed to get out and do something not wedding related. Kat found it."

"Interesting. Well, I'm sorry about those two dicks. Those kind of people don't usually get let in."

"It's fine. We handled it."

"I have no doubt in my mind you could have. Want me to leave?" I acted like I was going to get up and go.

She grabbed my arm in a death grip. "No. Stay. Please. I'm really glad you're here."

I sat back down. "Me too. I wasn't really going to leave you. It's taken me a long time to get you to myself. I'll take every moment I can get at this point, I'm noy gonna chance it."

She smiled timidly, and I loved that she seemed to still feel shy around me. "Thank you for that, not leaving me, I mean."

We sat for a while in comfortable silence, except for the low humming of chatter around the room and instrumental background music.

"So, I guess you're officially ditching your friend for me, or do you plan on getting back to your regularly scheduled program?"

It pained me that Chloe would even think I would abandon her for whatever the hell it was she thought I'd rather be doing. "He'll be just fine on his own." I brushed a stray curl out of her face. "I'd much rather be sitting here than anything else I could be doing."

She looked genuinely surprised by my admission. "How come? Not up for it?"

*You have no idea.* "No, not at all. And I planned on bailing early again tonight, then you showed up."

"Why would you leave early? You didn't even know I was going to be here."

"Honestly? I needed some form of confirmation for myself that whatever this is that's been happening lately is real." I took her hand in mine. "That this certain someone who has kept me distracted and questioning my life's goals isn't just all in my head." For the most part, I knew it wasn't, but I wanted lay it all out there and hopefully hear her take on it.

She sat quietly for a minute, letting my words sink in. "But—wait, what? Are you talking about me?"

Well, here goes nothing. "Chloe, ever since I left you in Vegas, it's been life as usual for me for the most part. Don't get me wrong, I've had my moments here and there where I thought things were going to go back to normal. But I've spent more time wondering if I'd ever see you again, even though I doubted I would. But you're here with me now by some crazy act of the universe. That has to mean something. Don't you think?"

"Well—I—yeah, I do. I mean, you're not the only one who's thought about us or this or whatever it is. But how would anything ever work between us? We practically live two worlds apart."

I laughed quietly to myself as I stared down at her hand still in mine. She wasn't entirely wrong. "I didn't say I wanted to marry you again, Chloe. I just know how we are when we're together and how much more amazing we could be if we ever get the chance. But when you leave here next week, we can keep in touch even if it's only by text and see how it goes…or not at all if that's what you want."

She stared down at her drink before looking up at me. "I don't know what I want anymore. But you

182

know damned well I don't mind at least hooking up while I'm here…or at least trying. That's all I ever wanted to do from the beginning."

I rubbed the back of my neck. I guessed hooking up was a start and not necessarily a bad one. "I can respect that, and I appreciate your honesty. But if we're being brutally honest here—" I leaned over to whisper in her ear "—if it makes you feel any better, I still have the unrelenting urge to bend you over, snatch that tight little skirt over your ass, and claim you as mine from behind. Maybe we'll make *that* our start."

She shivered from head to toe. *That's my girl.*

"Where would we go if I were any other girl you'd picked here and taken to bed? Back to your place?"

Reluctantly, I let go of her hand as I sat up and took a sip of my beer. "No, actually. I've never taken anyone back to my place. Not in a long time. Usually we go to their place or somewhere close by."

"I'd offer up a solution, but I got none. Plus, I can't get away from Kat long enough for her to not notice, much less leave her alone."

I leaned back in my barstool and craned my neck to peek behind the wall blocking my view. "Something tells me your friend would be just fine without you, and I hardly think she'd notice you were gone."

"What do you mean?" She gripped my thighs for support and leaned across me to get a look at what I'd been talking about. I wrapped my arms around her waist to hold her up. Then, without warning, I pulled her back, practically mouth to mouth with me.

"Hi."

"Hey," she whispered back. "Can I, um, help you with something?"

I smiled at her. "Oh, you have no idea." I skimmed my lips across hers. As soon as she closed her eyes, Katie's voice cracked through the air.

"Break it up. We gotta go."

Chloe jolted upright. "What the—? Why? What's wrong?"

"It's Rowan," Warren said, standing close behind Katie. "I just got a text from Wes; he's taking her to the hospital."

"What? The hospital? Why?"

"We don't know. He just said he needed to take her in but for us not to worry."

Chloe grabbed her purse, I threw some cash on the counter to cover our tab, and we all made our way outside.

"How far is the hospital from here?" Chloe asked no one in particular.

I wrapped my arms around her, pulling her into a hug from behind, hoping to reassure her everything

184

would be okay, even though I had no idea what the hell was going on. "Ten minutes? I already sent for an Uber."

# TWENTY

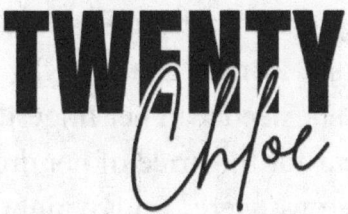

*Chloe*

The first longest week of my life was that one time I waited for Mother Nature to pay me her monthly visit; the second was this past week waiting for Rowan's wedding.

Ever since Rowan's unexpected hospital visit, Kat and I had decided we were not going to leave her side until we had to physically get on a plane and fly back home...or at least until her wedding night. Thankfully, she only had to spend one night in the hospital for observation and some IV fluids. Turned out she wasn't giving us some bullshit excuse about being on antibiotics so she wouldn't have to drink with us. Unfortunately, the meds just weren't strong enough. But we were glad to have her home, safe, and back to feeling like herself.

Once Rowan had all of us convinced she was *fine* and Wesley let her off bed rest a few days later, we were finally able to get out and go get our dresses. As promised, the shop had everything we'd needed. We helped Rowan pick out her dress, and *holy shit*. When I saw the price tag, I knew exactly why that dress shop had everything she needed at her fingertips. I could have bought a new car for the price of her dress.

Now here we were, Friday night before my best friend's big day, her last few hours as a bachelorette, and as that unwanted pang of jealousy crept up, I squashed it down just as fast because I was genuinely happy for her. She was going to be a stunning bride and make an even better wife. She deserved happiness just as much as anyone else.

"Where's Camilla at tonight?" Katie asked Rowan as we sat in our pj's, curled up on different areas of Wesley's massive sectional, drinking wine. "I figured she'd be here tonight."

Rowan gave a slight eye roll—that did not go unnoticed—and chugged back some of her bottled water. "I invited her, but she didn't sound interested. I just told her since we had pretty much ironed out all the details earlier this week, and she got her dress, she didn't need to feel obligated to hang out with boring old us."

*Thank fuck.* "Honestly, I'm glad she isn't here," I said. "Something about her doesn't sit right with me." Okay, so nothing about her sat right with me, and most of it had to do with Daniel—maybe all of it had to do with him. I was just glad to know he wasn't out and about doing his *regular* thing. He was with Wesley, Shane, and Warren at Warren's place, which just happened to be a few floors below us. So, as far as I knew, everyone had stayed in and behaved themselves. Plus, Daniel had been sending me some highly inappropriate and very much welcomed saucy text messages. All we had to do was somehow make each one of his dirty promises come to fruition…in less than thirty-six hours.

Wishful thinking at this point.

"I like her okay," Katie said, perking up. "But I haven't had much to do with her in the past two weeks. She kind of just makes her presence known, stays for a bit, then leaves. I guess as long as she shows up for the wedding tomorrow, that's all that matters."

"I hope so too. I don't think she'd bail, though. I mean, she'll have to see Wesley and Daniel at the hospital at some point. I can't imagine she wouldn't not show up to be in our wedding and then come into work Monday like nothing happened."

I absolutely could see her doing that. From what little I did know about her, she seemed shady enough and just gave me that feeling.

"What's your beef with her, Chlo? You've spent just as little time with her as I have...or am I missing something."

"You're missing something," Rowan said to Katie.

I looked at Rowan. "No she's not. What are you talking about?"

"Other than you and Daniel almost kissing at the bar last week, what did I miss?"

"Almost kissing?" Rowan practically spit out her water. "What in the hell did *I* miss? Spill it, Chloe."

*Shit, Katie.* "Okaaay. Apparently I'm the one missing something here. We did not almost kiss. And—"

"Oh, yes, you did. You two would have had your tongues down each other's throats if I hadn't walked up on you."

"Fine. We *almost* kissed. Almost doesn't count for a whole lotta nothing. And that's all we are—nothing."

"Well, by the way y'all have been looking at each other every time y'all are together, you can't tell me there's nothing going on there."

"Oh, I can and there's not."

"Hell, why not? He's fine as hell. I'd do him myself," Katie said. "But I just get the feeling he's all about him some Chloe. Plus, you need a good lay after that Tanner disaster."

She wasn't wrong. I did need a good lay. Hard and fast would win the race at this point. "I don't disagree with that, but I can assure you, there's nothing going on between me and Daniel." *I wish.* Oh, how I wished. Some days I wished even more that I'd just tell them about our history and get it out of the way.

"So what do you know, Rowan? You're the one who started this."

I wasn't entirely sure I even wanted to know what inside information Rowan had. For all I knew, Daniel had already told Wesley everything and he'd told Rowan. *Holy crap.* What if she already knew? Ohmigod. It never even crossed my mind that Daniel might have told someone already.

Rowan's eyes darted between me and Kat. "Sorry, Chloe. Cat's about to be out of the bag."

Well, so much for my big secret. So, me being my *don't think before you speak* self just blurted it out. "It's not like we were legally married."

Rowan dropped her open bottle of water on the floor; Katie choked on her wine.

"Do what?" they both shouted.

*Well, shit.*

After being grilled by the two of them for alllll the details, I'd finally confessed to my best friends everything from that night of the marathon that they'd left me to my own devices, up until now.

"Holy fucking shit. It all makes sense now," Rowan said.

"It does?" Katie asked, still obviously in shock at my admission to Daniel's and my fake shotgun wedding.

"Yeah. Well, most of it. Daniel has been acting…different. Ever since Chloe showed up. I knew something was up, but I never would have guessed it was *that*. I just thought he had a thing for you, and he and Camilla had a thing that he didn't know what to do with."

I took in a deep breath and blew it out. "They don't. Well, they did. Supposedly it was a long time ago, but she hasn't let him go since. He's promised me there's nothing there, and I want to believe him."

"Well, I told him last week at rehearsal lunch that whatever he had going on with her, he needed to end it before messing with you or I was going to kick his ass if he hurt you."

"Thanks for looking out, but I'm good. We're just talking. That's all. Trying to navigate things from here…I guess."

Rowan got up from the cozy nest of pillows and throw blankets she'd made for herself and hugged me. "Well, either way, whether it's Daniel or someone else,

I know there's someone perfect for you out there. Y'all are gonna find each other one way or the other."

"Yeah," Kat said, plopping herself down next to me. "Look at Rowan. She had to damn near killed her future husband. Then she moved halfway across the country to be with him."

Rowan tossed a throw pillow at Katie. "Give it time. Your prince will come."

Oh, he needed to come all right, and so did I.

♡♡♡

"Well, guys, it's go-time. Y'all ready?" Rowan said, smoothing her hands down the front of her princess wedding dress.

"Oh, we're ready, and you make a perfect bride," Kat said to Rowan, who stood solo waiting to walk down the aisle. "The question is, are you ready?"

Once I'd finished airing out all my dirty laundry to them, we spent the rest of the night girl-talking about people back at home, all our other crazy times we'd had together, and Rowan's big day. Now, seeing Rowan all decked out in her bridal gear, I couldn't help but for a quick moment think back on my own wedding night, if I could even call if that anymore. Maybe she was right, that my someone was out there. I just hadn't found him yet.

Lyndsay Marie

She clutched her bouquet of calla lilies and orchids in a death grip. "Never been more ready for anything in my life."

We were all finally standing place, waiting to walk down the aisle. Warren and Katie stood tall in front of me, pretty much blocking out my entire view of the rooftop. Shane and I were linked arm in arm behind them. I couldn't see Daniel or Camilla, but I could hear her, and I could smell him just behind me. Rowan waited behind a silk curtain backdrop just beyond them.

Instrumental music played as the usher drew back the white sheer curtains that separated us from the guests. Right before Kat and Warren were given the signal to walk, Daniel said something to Shane, and Shane let go of my arm and moved away. *What the—?* I didn't have time to ask what in the hell was going on before I realized that he and Daniel had swapped places. Daniel took my arm in his.

I pushed up on my tippy toes and whispered under my breath. "What are you doing?"

He smiled down at me. "Want me to go back?"

I gripped his arm tighter. "No. But Rowan is going to kill us."

He glanced back over his shoulder, probably looking in her direction. "Something tells me she won't mind." Then he leaned down and planted a kiss on my cheek.

193

We made it through the wedding without a hitch. Rowan and Wesley exchanged vows, said "I do," and danced their way back down the aisle to go live out their happily ever after.

The reception was just as over-the-top as anything I'd ever seen. I made a mental note to get the name and number of their decorator…just in case. Throughout the night, Daniel and I talked more openly and enjoyed each other's company. As the end of the night approached and the party died down, Katie, who had indulged herself in the open bar, had to literally be carried out by Warren. I somehow got volunteered to escort them back to his place.

A soft *ping* sounded as the elevator arrived and the doors slid open. I let Warren in first with Katie hanging in his arms. I stepped in behind them.

"Shit," I said as the doors started to close. "I forgot my clutch. It's got my wallet in it."

"Where is it?" Warren asked.

"I shoved it in the corner behind a bunch of totes we stashed away earlier. Do you think it'll be safe until morning?" The door started to close again, and I stuck my hand out, catching it.

"I'm sure it will, but go get it just to be safe. They'll have a crew here half the night cleaning up. Want us to wait?"

I stepped off the elevator. "No. I'll catch up with y'all."

"Don't take too long. Rowan will cut my balls off if I lose either of you. You remember where I live?"

I stuck my hand back inside the elevator and punched the button for his floor. "Yup. I'll be right there."

"I'll leave the door unlocked." The doors closed, and I made my way back down the long, carpeted hallway toward the reception area. I found my clutch and started making a beeline for the elevator.

"Leaving so soon?"

The sound of his voice stopped me dead in my tracks. Soft footsteps approached me from behind, and I felt the brush of warm fingertips across the back of my neck, pushing my hair to the side.

I swallowed hard. "I—I'm—Katie."

"Hmm. You're Chloe—" he pressed his lips to my bare shoulder, trailing kisses along my skin up to my neck "—but what about her?"

"Nothing." He wrapped his arm around my waist, pulling my back flush into his front. "Shit, Daniel."

"Katie is with Warren," he said, his breath warm against my skin. "She'll be just fine. He's harmless." His grip tightened across my waist, allowing me to feel the entire length of his hard dick in my back. "I'll text him and let him know you're in safe hands. And I promise I won't bite…hard," he said as he gently, but firmly bit into the side of my neck.

Instant. Turn. On.

As if I hadn't already been turned on and up to maximum capacity all week, his touch cranked my horniness level beyond anything I'd ever felt.

"Where exactly do you want to go?" I asked him, trying to catch my breath. "Everyone's place is full, including yours."

"Ah. You underestimate me, sweetheart. I made a promise to you, and I fully intend to keep it."

I reached my hand behind me and grabbed on to his thigh. "So…where are we going?"

"Back to my condo." He spun me around to face him. "Shane left with Camilla. We'll have the whole place all to ourselves. No more excuses, and no more interruptions." He put his hand under my chin, tilted my head up, and tenderly pressed his lips to mine. "Just you—" *Kiss.* "—and me—" *Kiss.* "—and nothing but the air between us."

I smiled at him, then reached between us, grabbed his dick, and gave it a firm squeeze. "Since I gave you the nine you claimed you'd earned at the pool, I think it's your turn to give me mine."

# TWENTY-ONE
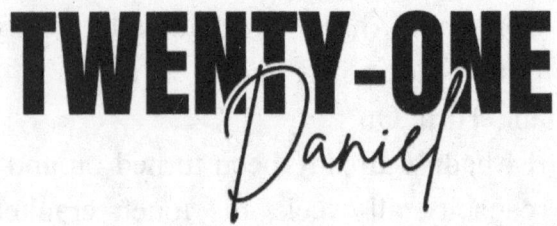
*Daniel*

It was Vegas all over again, except this time there was nothing to get in our way. We made it back to my place in record time, even though we almost didn't make it out of the parking garage to get here or out of my car after we'd parked.

This was finally fucking it. The shit we'd started over a year ago and fought for to happen for the last two weeks was about to go down.

I scooped Chloe up off her feet as we stepped off the elevator. She wrapped her arms around my neck as I carried her down the hall and into my condo. I flicked on the entryway light and kicked the door closed behind us.

As soon as we were in the foyer, I set her down. "I know I've told you before, but you are so fucking beautiful." I cupped her face in my hands, pulled her into me, and kissed her. She relaxed as she gave in and met my lips, movement for movement, our tongues sweeping across one another.

"This dress," I said as I traced my finger across her shoulder and down her arm, "this shade of blue, whatever it is, is really your color. But it would look so much better in a heap on the floor."

She bit her bottom lip. "Yeah? You think so?"

I leaned down and gently pulled her lip between my teeth, gently biting it. "Oh, I know." Then I spun her around to face the mirror hanging above the console table. "I'll prove it."

I slowly unzipped her dress, grazing my fingers along her spine, all the way down her back to the top of her ass. The satin dress fell like water to the floor.

She stepped out of it, pushing it to the side.

I sucked in a deep breath. "Fuck." I wanted to ravage her body and savor every inch of her at the same time.

"Like what you see?"

Considering she hadn't been wearing a bra *or* panties all damned night, apparently, there was no way in hell I could *not* like what I had in front of me. "You already know I do."

I locked eyes with her in the mirror as I loosened the tie around my neck and slipped it off. She licked her lips and gripped the console table as she bent forward and gave her luscious bare ass a shake.

"Tease." My dick strained against my pants. I needed to get them off, but first thing's first. I rested my palm on her lower back, holding her in place. Then with my free hand, I smacked her ass. "Hope you don't mind being spanked."

She looked back at me, staring me dead in the eyes. "Try harder next time."

"You're fucking killing me, Chloe." I moved my hand from her ass cheek to the inside of her thigh and cupped her hot pussy. She spread her legs apart as I slid my fingers between her lips, stroking her from front to back. I withdrew my hand and backed away from her.

"Wha—what are you doing?" she said breathlessly. "Don't stop."

"Oh, I'm just getting started. There's only so much I can do to you with my clothes on." I undid my dress shirt one button at time, making sure she was watching me, pulled my T-shirt off over my head, and undressed until my clothes were on the floor beside her dress and I was completely naked.

She hadn't moved an inch.

I stepped up behind her and wedged my dick between her legs and slowly pressed against her entrance, ever so slightly sliding inside of her. She tried pushing back against me, but I gripped her hips and steadied her. "Nice try."

Then I flipped her around and picked her up. She wrapped her arms around my neck and her legs around my waist as I positioned the head of my dick against her fiery slick heat. With my arms holding her tight around her waist, I pulled her down onto me, sliding all the way deep inside of her.

She moaned my name, and I almost busted a nut right then and there.

I did everything I could to pull her up and down on my dick as I walked us toward the bed. Fucking and walking was a lot harder than it seemed my mind. But I was no quitter.

Once I made it to my bed, I laid her down on the edge, still buried inside of her, and started pounding into her. As much as I wanted to take my time and savor every second, time was of the essence, and my orgasm was not going to wait.

Neither was hers.

She reached her hands over her head, gripping and pulling at the comforter. She was trying to speak, but her words were ragged and breathless.

I leaned down on top of her and took one of her peaked nipples into my mouth and sucked. She let out a yelp, then threaded her fingers through my hair, coaxing me for more.

I reached between us and stroked her clit. That was all it took. She tightened so hard around my dick I thought she was going to pull it off. I pulsed inside of her and let out a long, loud moan that I'd been holding in just for the sake of wanting to hear her scream.

♡♡♡

Hooking up with Chloe would forever be my favorite highlight of the year. I held her in my arms with her head on my chest as I played with her hair in post-coital bliss after round two.

"You know, I never did respond to your text message?"

She glanced up at me in confusion. "You didn't? Which one?

"The first one you ever sent me."

"You mean from last Friday when I asked you what you were doing? That one?

"Yeah, that one. I never responded to you."

"Actually you kind of did," she said as she drew circles on my stomach with her fingertips. "You showed up out of nowhere and saved me from those gross dudes. I'd say that was a pretty damned good response."

"True, but that wasn't good enough."

"Okay, then. Reply now. What are you doing?"

"Falling for you."

## The End...(almost).

# EPILOGUE
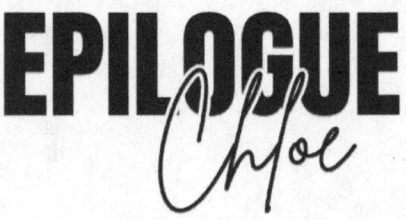
*Chloe*

While Daniel and I had had the times of our lives after Rowan and Wesley's big day, I still had to go home. It was back to life as usual for me and Daniel, sort of. Only this time when we parted ways, we had each other's phone numbers and stayed in touch daily.

Except life as normal didn't last very long—for either of us.

I decided to take a huge leap of faith and put in a request to change positions within my company. I knew after I left Chicago that I needed something with a little more freedom and flexibility than just working from home and popping into the office once or twice a week. As nice as that was, I wanted something more out of life and work. Specifically, I wanted to get out of Memphis, even if it was just temporarily for work. Katie had always talked about doing the same thing, more so after

Rowan had done it, but she didn't know when or how to pull the trigger or tell her parents.

The decision to venture away was a lot easier for me.

After a couple of weeks of waiting, my boss finally sent me a list of openings, and I took my first assignment in—drumroll please—Chicago! When I'd told Daniel about my new promotion and that I was coming up to his part of town for work, he offered me a place to sleep while I was there, even though my room and board were paid for by my company. He insisted I stay with him and I didn't fight him too hard on it…or at all.

I wasn't planning on staying in Chicago forever.

What was supposed to be a couple of days turned into a couple of months. Daniel's offer for me a place to stay while I worked went from *it'll be a friends-only living arrangement*, to us fucking like rabbit's day and night, starting from the minute we'd walked through the door after he picked me up from the airport on my first day there. I wasn't sure if he was happier to see me or his sport jacket that I returned to him in the same condition when he'd left me with it.

"How's your latest article coming along? Need any help?" Daniel asked me from across the room. *Our bedroom.*

He loved helping me research restaurants for me to write about. Even better, was sometimes he was able to take off work and travel with me on my assignments. "Actually, I think I would like a travel buddy on this one, but it's not local."

"Of course I'll go with you—be your bodyguard and personal sex slave." He stood butt naked just out of my reach and flexed his muscles while swinging his hard dick back and forth. That shit would never get old. *He* would never get old. "Just say when and I'll make sure to take off work."

I bit my bottom lip. "Well, that might be a *slight* problem."

He walked over and curled up beside me in the bed and pressed his naked body flush against mine while looking at my laptop screen. "What's the problem?"

"It's in Vegas."

He glanced up at me. "No shit? Vegas, huh? So? We've been to Vegas before." He placed his hand on my bare thigh and slid it upward. *Holy hell.* I wasn't going to get shit done if he got any closer to my—. *Damn it.* He rubbed the thin piece of cotton fabric that prevented his deft fingers from very easily sliding inside of me. My breathing grew heavier the harder he rubbed. I knew exactly how this was going to end. "Chloe? Talk to me."

"Yeah, I—I'm thinking."

His touch was firm and purposeful and of course I couldn't focus on anything else when Daniel was working me into an orgasm. He kissed the top of my thigh as he rubbed…and rubbed and rubbed, until his fingers finally found their way beneath my panties and skimmed over the slick puddle forming between my legs.

He sucked in air. "Fuck, Chloe. You never disappoint me."

"Hmm." I slammed my laptop shut and tossed it beside me in the bed. Then I lay back, giving him more room to work with. Damned if I was gonna get shit for work done today. He'd fried the brain cells that kept me productive.

"Hmm." He mirrored my moans while kissing my hip bone, up my stomach, before lifting my shirt up and sucking my hard nipple as he slowly finger-fucked me at the same time. "So, when are we going to Vegas?"

It was all I could do to keep from coming on his hand because I wanted—no, needed—him inside of me. I fisted my hand in his hair, pulling him up to kiss me. Aside from his magical penis, his lips and mouth were my favorite parts of him.

"Next week," I said into his mouth as we kissed. He climbed over me, pulled my panties to the side, never breaking our kiss, and finally glided his magic stick all of the way inside of me. I hooked my leg around him and pulled him down into me as far as he could go.

He pinned my hands over my head. "I'll come with you…after I make you come."

…One Week Later…

My stomach was in knots as our plane landed in Las Vegas. So much had changed since the last time we were here, all for the better, but that didn't calm the sea of nerves that raged out of control.

The first thing we did as soon as we'd got our things settled in our hotel room was hit the Strip and search out this new restaurant. I skimmed over the info I'd printed out, punched in the address on my phone, and led the way. The butterflies in my stomach settled slightly as we walked and were replaced with excitement and anticipation of checking out this location. It was a fairly new place that'd opened up a few weeks ago, so their website didn't have much to offer since it was still under construction.

We walked a few blocks, rounded the corner, and stopped dead in front of a familiar building. I looked up at sign hanging over the door, down at my phone, then back up at the sign. "I'm confused. Isn't this the ice cream shop we came to when we were here?"

Daniel looked up with me. "Huh. Sure looks like it. We were feeling pretty good, though." He smirked. "Let's go in and find out."

He held the pink wooden door open and followed me through. The smell of sugar, butter, and popcorn smacked my senses. "It smells amazing in here. I guess this is it." I knew it was a gourmet popcorn place I was looking for; I just hadn't realized it *was* still the same ice cream shop. They'd just added popcorn to their menu and renovated the establishment.

We introduced ourselves to the owners, who were hard at work behind the glass counter making what looked like at least a dozen different confectionery popcorn treats and mixing ice cream flavors. They invited us to join them for a break at one of the recently added booths along the wall. After spending the next hour talking with them, we realized that they not only had bought the ice cream shop, but they were the owners of the popcorn truck that Daniel and I had stopped by on the way into the wedding chapel. They'd since given up the truck and combined their gourmet popcorn and new ice cream shop into one business.

We thanked them for their time as we gathered up our things. "Well, where to now?"

Daniel wrapped his arm around me, pulling me into his side, and kissed my cheek. "Hmm. We still have plenty of time. I'll let you pick first. Because once I get you back to that hotel room, we aren't leaving until we have to."

"I like the way you think, but I thought we might do a little sightseeing in the daytime."

"I'll wait if I must. What'd you have in mind?"

"Well, I know of a little pink wedding chapel not far from here. We could grab us a bag of popcorn on the way out and go check things out…you know? For old times' sake?"

He rubbed his chin. "Actually," he said, taking my laptop bag from off my shoulder and setting it down on the table. "There is something I want to do while we're here."

"Okay…what's that?"

He stood, facing me, and held both of my hands in his. "Chloe. I love you."

"I—I love you too, Daniel. But what's wrong?"

He smiled. "Nothing's wrong. Unless you say no."

"No to what?"

He let go of my hands and dropped down on one knee, reaching into his pocket. He pulled out a very obvious black velvet box.

"Holy shit."

"Chloe Grace Hill, marry me?" He swallowed hard. "This time I mean it."

Tears blurred my vision, but I knew without a doubt Daniel was who I wanted for the rest of my life.

He waited patiently, down on one knee in front of me for me to give him an answer

I wiped the tears from my cheeks then dove into his arms. "Yes. Yes! Always yes."

He held me for a minute before pulling me back to slip the ring on my finger. The owners had witnessed the whole thing and were cheering from across the room.

I stared down at my new engagement ring and watched as the diamond sparkled under the fluorescent lighting. "I love it, Daniel. And I love you."

He gave me a gentle kiss. "I love you, too. More than anything. But I have one more question for you."

"Okay…what's that?"

"You wanna go check out that pink wedding chapel?

# ONE
## Jameson

"What the hell do you mean he got away?" I bit out.

This was the second time in less than a week that one of Kane's idiot men had almost gotten inside my casino. It was bad enough they even made it onto the property, much less halfway down the corridor and practically out onto the gaming floor.

Okay, maybe not quite that far, but it still felt too close for comfort.

The line fell silent.

With the telephone clutched in a death grip pressed against my ear, I gazed up at Ivan. I watched him as he sat there just as casually as could be across from me with a dumbfounded *don't ask me* look plastered on his face.

"Answer me," I demanded with a huff. My words were directed at Chris, Emerald Haze's general operations manager. Ivan knew I was talking to him, too.

"Yeah, James," he breathed defeatedly. "I'm here. I don't—I don't fucking know how. He ran out and got away from us before we could catch up to him. Leon took a pop at him, but the guy slipped through the woods on the south side."

"Unbelievable. Did anyone see or hear Leon shoot?"

"Not that I'm aware of. He used his silencer. Again, I'm so sorry. I know we fucked up."

"You think? I've got Kane's men creeping and crawling around this place like flies on horse shit, and *you*, of all people, almost welcomed them in with open arms and a cup of tea."

I'd given all my men one simple order: stop anyone who isn't supposed to be here in their tracks and stop them at all costs—it didn't matter where or how.

That's it.

That's all they had to do these days. I didn't think that was too much to ask for.

"Y'all have one job. One. Fucking. Job, Chris. Do I need to start doing this shit myself?" I wouldn't. But I was getting close to it.

"No," he sighed. "Again, I'm sorry."

"Sorry doesn't fix it. Bullets do." Even though a bullet was what had gotten me into this clusterfuck in the first place.

As much as I hated death and dying, I'd long accepted that killing was a necessary evil in this business. Sometimes that meant kill or be killed. We all had enemies in this industry, and unfortunately, my dad's had been passed down to me. Kane was only

212

going to hold off for so long before saying *fuck it* and ripping off the proverbial Band-Aid.

I had less than a week before said ripping occurred.

I massaged my forehead in an attempt to ward off an impending migraine, then let out a slow, deep breath, trying to calm my nerves and collect my thoughts before opening my mouth to speak—an art I'd yet to perfect.

"Is everyone else okay?" I asked because even when my guys messed up, which wasn't very often, I still cared about them. The last thing I wanted was for anyone else to get hurt or end up dead.

One was already enough.

"Yeah, we're all good," Chris reassured. "Everyone's fine."

"Good. Don't let them that close again."

"Yes, ma'am."

"Thank you. Now, get back to work." I slammed the phone down on the receiver, ending the call.

I already knew everyone thought I was a t-total bitch, but a job like this wasn't meant for the soft and weak. I'd spent the majority of my life being conditioned for this role—to be callous and coldhearted.

I wasn't about to let them prove me wrong now.

"James." Ivan rubbed the back of his neck.

"What?"

"Go easy on our guys. You know we're all feeling the pressure here, right?"

"There won't be any more *guys* left to feel the pressure if my crew lets any more of these assholes get away. At this point, I want to see bodies stacked up to the goddamned sky. I don't even give a shit where we dispose of them anymore. Throw them out in Kane's parking lot. Let his patrons use them as speed bumps for all I care."

I plopped down onto my executive leather office chair and pulled up the security cameras that covered the exterior perimeter of the property. I did a quick scan of the south side of the property, where the perp had been chased.

Nothing.

The sun was shining, and the grass was brown but still had a smattering of green coloring left to it here and there. Trees had lost most of their leaves.

It was as though he'd never been here.

"These guys are getting entirely too close for my comfort." They'd mostly stayed away from me until recently. Now, they were popping up left and right. None had gotten as close as the one today, and he'd somehow managed to make it all the way through the front door.

In their defense, it was getting harder and harder to spot these guys. They'd come in through the main entrance, and if not for my keen-eyed surveillance crew or the extensive research IT did on Kane and his circus, we'd be none the wiser as to who they were or their intentions.

But my men? Oh, they knew.

Lyndsay Marie

"I agree. That's why I keep telling you we need help."

I stared Ivan down through squinted eyes. "No. We do not. We can handle this ourselves."

"Yes, we do, and no, we cannot. James. You're—" He paused, scrubbing his hands down his face. He was clearly just as sick of my shit as everyone else around here. "You're in way over your head, and forgive me for what I'm about to say, but you're hardheaded as fuck. I know that's not what you wanna hear, but it's—"

I held up my hand to stop him. "Save it. I already know what you're going to say. You, of all people, know how damn near impossible it is to find someone— anyone—we can trust. You're not just gonna pull some Joe Blow off the streets of Tunica or Memphis and expect him to do what you or any of us do. That's what Kane does, and he's sloppy for doing it."

"I don't disagree, but please, hear me out."

I closed my eyes, waiting to hear what he had to say, even though I didn't want to hear another word about needing help.

"I might know someone."

"Might? What do you mean you *might* know someone?" Ivan *might* know someone? This was news to me.

"Okay, okay." He waved his hands dismissively. "Relax. I *know* a guy. Better?"

"No, not at all." There was a substantial difference between just knowing someone and having them readily available to put their life at risk. Those were two completely different things. "Look, Ivan. I've got Kane's men crawling

Continue reading Trust Fall here—
https://www.amazon.com/dp/B0DYWXRM8L

Lyndsay Marie

www.AuthorLyndsayMarie.com

Visit me on Amazon —
https://www.amazon.com/author/lyndsaymarie

www.ingramcontent.com/pod-product-compliance
Lightning Source LLC
Chambersburg PA
CBHW011516100726
47899CB00010BD/3393